Praise for
The Pregnant Pause

"Jane Doucet has hit the nail on the head and will clip your funny bone along the way with her debut novel, *The Pregnant Pause*. From mommy friends with foot-in-mouth digs to a mother-in-law's not-so-subtle hints, Jane's entertaining and insightful look at baby fever is a terrific blend of humour and relatability. If you keep hitting the snooze button on your biological clock, *The Pregnant Pause* needs to be your bed-side reading!"

LAURA EARL
radio host and star of *I'm an Army Wife...Now What?*

"It's a babypalooza, and Rose isn't sure she wants to buy a ticket. But her clock is counting down, and as she struggles with her ambivalence in a baby-obsessed world, she discovers that one size does not fit all—and the only right choice is the one she makes. *The Pregnant Pause* is a thoughtful, honest and poignant exploration of how motherhood continues to define us as women, and it invites us to recognize that we are our sisters' keepers."

CHARLOTTE EMPEY
former editor-in-chief, *Canadian Living*

"In Rose, Jane Doucet gives voice to the archetypal working woman staring down the barrel of forty as she wrestles with the angst of whether she and her husband are cut out to be parents. As she weighs the should-we-or-shouldn't-we decision, she sifts through the events of her life and those around her like a clairvoyant reading tea leaves. In the process, we see Rose grow and, dare I say, bloom."

JANICE BIEHN
former editor-in-chief, *ParentsCanada*

Praise for
Fishnets & Fantasies

"I haven't had this much fun reading a book in a long time.... Irreverent, wise, and more than a bit cheeky, *Fishnets & Fantasies* is an absolute delight."

AMY JONES
bestselling author of *We're All In This Together*

"The spirit of Stephen Leacock meets a colourful pantheon of contemporary Nova Scotia characters simmering in a sexually charged Lunenburg pheromone chowder!"

RON JAMES
award-winning comedian, actor, and author of *All Over the Map*

"[*Fishnets & Fantasies*] proves prolific journalist Jane Doucet can write a very funny novel.... Peopled with believable characters...hilarious plot points and fun storytelling, it's meant to transport you not to a sunny California beach, but a wild Atlantic shore."

TORONTO STAR

"Jane Doucet has a flare for writing the inner dialogue of characters as they struggle through their triumphs and challenges.... Well-paced, funny, and full of slap-stick comedy, this book makes perfect reading."

THE MIRAMICHI READER

"*Fishnets & Fantasies* is gutsy, cheeky, and full of laughs. Jane Doucet has created characters who are real enough to step out of the pages and join you for a nice glass of pinot noir.... You're going to have a ball!"

BETTE MACDONALD
award-winning actor and comedian

"Want a sassy good time and a great giggle? Make a date with *Fishnets & Fantasies*."

LESLEY CREWE
Globe and Mail bestselling author of *Nosy Parker*

The Pregnant Pause

Jane Doucet

Vagrant PRESS

Vagrant Press is an imprint of
Nimbus Publishing Limited
3660 Strawberry Hill Street, Halifax, NS, B3K 5A9
(902) 455-4286 nimbus.ca

Printed and bound in Canada

NB1666

This story is a work of fiction. Names, characters, incidents, and places, including organizations and institutions, are used fictitiously.

Editor: Elizabeth Eve

Editor for the press: Whitney Moran

Design: Jenn Embree

Library and Archives Canada Cataloguing in Publication

Title: The pregnant pause / Jane Doucet.
Names: Doucet, Jane, 1968- author.
Description: Previously published: Halifax, Nova Scotia:
All My Words, 2017.
Identifiers: Canadiana (print) 20220457646
Canadiana (ebook) 20220457654 | ISBN 9781774711606 (softcover)
ISBN 9781774711613 (EPUB)
Classification: LCC PS8607.O9143 P74 2023 | DDC C813/.6—dc23

Canada NOVA SCOTIA Canada Council Conseil des arts
for the Arts du Canada

Nimbus Publishing acknowledges the financial support for its publishing activities from the Government of Canada, the Canada Council for the Arts, and from the Province of Nova Scotia. We are pleased to work in partnership with the Province of Nova Scotia to develop and promote our creative industries for the benefit of all Nova Scotians.

For me, and for other women
who would have liked to have had children

One

SHORTLY BEFORE ROSE AINSWORTH'S THIRTY-seventh birthday everything went to shit. In a few weeks she'd be leaving thirty-six behind, which is not so old to someone who is eighty, but for some reason Rose was having a hard time accepting the inevitability of thirty-seven.

Rose used to shake her head when younger friends became fearful as their thirtieth birthday approached. "Thirty is great!" she'd trill happily. "Thirty is about confidence. It's liberating." Or at least that was how she felt when she turned thirty. So why did she feel threatened by thirty-seven?

Maybe it had something to do with the fact that the night before, as Rose and her husband, Jim, were lying naked on their bed, about to begin their usual ten minutes of foreplay, he made a startling discovery.

"You've got a little belly," he announced out of the blue.

"I do *not* have a little belly," she retorted.

"Yes, you do—look," he said, poking his right index finger into what not so long ago had been Rose's taut midriff. "See, right there."

Rose looked in the direction of Jim's extended finger, and sure enough, her once-muscular stomach did indeed have some softness.

"Thanks for pointing that out," Rose said dryly, trying to inject enough sarcasm into her tone for Jim to get that she wasn't thrilled about his discovery, nor the fact that he had chosen such a poor time to mention it. But as she had learned after three years, two months, eleven days, and some irrelevant number of seconds of marriage, he wasn't going to get it.

Rose was right. Jim replied, "You're welcome" and returned to his husbandly duties—which, by now, she was no longer interested in.

Rose knew that it wasn't really her belly blubber that was bothering her. She was a health editor at a women's fitness magazine called *Dash*, the title of which is symbolic of "reaching the finish line of the many goals in women's fast-paced lives," according to the editorial mission statement. Rose knew that if she did stomach crunches, the soft flesh around her middle would be toned again. Since stomach crunches bored her to tears, however, it wasn't going to happen.

What was really bothering Rose was babies. Not hers, because she didn't have any. Other people's. And not just any other people's, but babies who belonged to women she knew and who, before they had babies, were friends. Good friends.

Rose had two nieces and a nephew, ages seven, five, and two, respectively: the offspring of Daisy, her older sister, and her husband, Steve, a radiologist she met when she worked as a nurse. They lived in Bedford, a suburb of Halifax and a two-hour flight from Toronto, while Rose and Jim lived in Cabbagetown. Rose loved those little people with all of her heart. She loved them when they were newborns who drooled, peed, and spit up on her, then as toddlers taking their first steps. She'd continue to love them when they turned into surly teenagers with bad skin, bad attitudes, and bad taste in music.

Or at least Rose hoped she'd still love them then. As long as they didn't come to her for money or drugs, or both.

Not only did Rose love those children, she also liked them. They were funny and clever. Except when they picked their noses and ate the contents in front of her or asked, "Do you want to play with me?" for the four hundredth time in five minutes, to which she'd reply: "Auntie Rose is tired. Auntie Rose can't play nonstop with stuffed animals like you can. Now get your Auntie Rose a beer and buzz off!"

Rose didn't actually say that last bit—Daisy wouldn't approve—but after the kids went to bed she often helped herself to a bottle or two if it had been a particularly challenging visit. On rare occasions she might have three—one for each child—and render herself unconscious. Mostly, though, she didn't have to drink at all when she was around them because they were so much fun. Tiring and smelly, but fun. And because they lived far away, she didn't see them as often as she wished.

When Rose started dating Jim, she asked him if he wanted children. He said that he hadn't thought about it. He was twenty-five at the time, five years younger than she was. Rose told him that she couldn't keep seeing him if he wasn't at least open to the idea. Then one night after a party and too many pints, he got sappy and said he *could* picture them with a family. Three years later they got married, and Rose got caught up in her life as a newlywed with a busy career, putting babies on the back burner.

Until recently, when Rose had started to think about them. Constantly. She began asking herself, "Do I want to have a baby?" But no matter how many times she posed the question, she couldn't come up with a definitive answer. She diagnosed herself with a first-time case of baby fever. She hoped it wasn't going to develop into a chronic condition and that there was something she could take to make it go away.

At that point Rose wasn't willing to fork out a hundred and eighty dollars for an hour of her therapist's time. She had long since maxed out her partially covered health-insurance allotment of three visits a year following upsetting incidents with her mother, so she decided to try analyzing herself.

Without professional help, this was as clear a picture as she could get. As long as Rose was thirty-six, she felt young. The only internal clock she had was the one that woke her up every morning at ten minutes to seven, before the alarm went off. As far as biological clocks went, she didn't hear any ticking. Which was perfect, because it absolved her of having to think about conception. If she decided down the road that she wanted a baby, she still had a few years. She knew plenty of women who had given birth for the first time between the ages of forty and forty-five. She could be one of those, too. Right?

Wrong. Or at least, not exactly right. As she was starting to figure out, nothing is quite that straightforward when it comes to having babies.

Rose knew that many of her friends—especially the single ones who were around her age and suffering from both marriage and baby fever—were shaking their heads and thinking, "What's her problem? She's married, she should just have a baby. What's stopping her from getting knocked up?"

Lots of things. First of all, Rose and Jim were living in a tiny two-bedroom apartment above a hardware store at a noisy corner in a busy city. They had a big deck, but it was surrounded by brick—the brick wall of a bank on one side and the brick wall of their neighbour's apartment on the other. It overlooked a grungy back alleyway. Rose didn't feel that it was a homey enough place in which to raise a child.

Then there were the stairs leading up to their apartment— eighteen of them, and steep to boot. Just thinking about lugging a stroller under one arm while balancing a baby on the opposite hip made her feel tired, sore, and cranky.

Plus, where would they put a baby? Sure, they had two bedrooms, but theirs was small and the other was an office, because Rose sometimes worked from home. It had the usual furniture: desk, chair, computer, printer, filing cabinet, bookcase, shelving units, recycling bin.

It also had a comfortable new sofa bed for overnight guests, which Rose supposed they could sell and replace with a crib. They had just bought it to replace a lumpy old futon, but having a baby would necessitate lifestyle sacrifices, right?

Buying a house wasn't an option because the previous year, Jim had decided to switch careers from teaching geography at a junior high school to writing advertising copy. While Rose wasn't entirely pleased with this change in direction, she tried to be supportive, after having several serious discussions when she asked him if he had lost his mind. How did he think they were going to pay their bills and save for a house on her meager publishing salary combined with his staggering drop in wages? He faithfully promised that it would only be a setback for a year or two.

Because Jim was friendly with the father of one of his students who owned a successful advertising agency, he was now working in an entry-level copywriting job that he loved despite being paid peanuts. Logically, Rose knew that you could raise a baby in an apartment—many people do, with astounding success—but she didn't want to join that club.

Rose figured that, since she was raised in Wolfville, a small town in Nova Scotia, with a backyard big enough for Daisy and her to run around in, then her baby must also have space, grass, and fresh air. In fact, she reflected, her childhood was great—until she turned seventeen and couldn't wait to move away to a big city full of brick walls.

Lately, Rose had been spending her spare time trying to come up with a formula that would tell her when exactly would be the right time for her to have a baby, if Jim eventually agreed, which she was (almost) certain he would with gentle persuasion.

If they budgeted hard for the next three years, they could afford a five per cent down payment on a fixer-upper—basically, the ugliest house with a postage-stamp-size backyard on a nice street in a residential neighbourhood on the outskirts of the downtown core but technically not in the suburbs, which would give Rose hives. They might even be able to buy a cheap used car.

Their monthly mortgage payments would be massive and, like their friends with houses and cars who also weren't independently wealthy—which was all of them—they would be up to their eyeballs in debt.

If that plan worked out, according to this timetable, Rose would be forty when they moved into their first house. Do you know what the statistics are of having no trouble conceiving a healthy baby at forty? Or conceiving at all? Exactly. Every time Rose thought about it, she returned to her calculation table and tried to revise it. Because if she was going to have one baby, she figured she should have two, given how close she and Daisy were.

The only thing Rose was sure about was that she didn't want to start trying to conceive after forty, when the odds were stacked against her getting pregnant and toward her miscarrying or having a baby with a life-threatening birth defect. In which case, she had to consider the possibility of giving birth while she and Jim were living in their apartment. As far as she could figure, it would mean adjusting the formula so she would try to be pregnant at thirty-nine. Could she handle three of them being crammed into their apartment, even for a year or two? Were they even allowed to have a baby there? They couldn't have pets, so she'd have to check the rental agreement.

Rose just didn't know. Usually she was a decisive person, but when it came to making baby-related decisions, she was as confused as you could get.

If one more person told Rose that there was no "right time" to have a baby—that unless you were expecting a sudden windfall of $100,000 in any given year, you would never have enough money to support one so you might as well go ahead and get pregnant—she would tear out their tongue with her bare hands. It was easy for them to say, what with their minivans and four-bedroom houses with three bathrooms in the suburbs. They already had it all, and Rose had—well, not much, if not exactly nothing.

Another line Rose heard frequently from women who had had their babies in their late thirties was, "If I'd known how great motherhood was, I would have started years ago."

"But you didn't, did you?" Rose felt like spewing. "And obviously you had good reasons for waiting, like maybe you didn't meet your partner until you were in your thirties or you had a hard time conceiving or you had to put your career first because your bum of a husband was unemployed."

Did Rose say any of that? Of course not. The one thing she had learned is that you can't tell a parent anything about children if you don't have any of your own. If you do, they'll look at you with a noxious mix of superiority and pity that makes you feel as though your life isn't worth living.

But it is, of course. That's what Rose kept telling herself, because no one else was.

Two

THREE RECENT EVENTS CONTRIBUTED TO ROSE'S baby fever. Life started to get lopsided when her friend Michelle had her first baby last year. Michelle didn't like children, but her husband, Shawn, wanted them. Apparently his enthusiasm was infectious—either that or the condom broke—because one day, much to Rose's surprise, at thirty-eight and after ten years of marriage, Michelle announced that she was pregnant.

On the evening in question, Rose and Michelle had made plans to meet for a drink after Michelle finished with her last patient at the massage therapy clinic where she worked. She told Rose she wouldn't be able to drink any alcohol because she was on antibiotics for an ear infection. Since Rose rarely drank, except on holiday, that didn't pose a problem. They met at their favourite restaurant and settled into a quiet corner booth.

"How's your ear?" Rose asked.

"Much better," Michelle replied, grinning. "Okay, I have to fess up or my head will explode. I don't have an ear infection—I'm pregnant!"

"That's amazing!" Rose shouted, scurrying around the table to hug her friend. For the rest of the evening, Michelle filled in the blanks: when she conceived (after a costume party that she and Shawn had hosted where she was Raggedy Ann and he was Raggedy Andy, which was creepy when Rose thought about it, so she tried not to), when she was due (end of February), how she was feeling (tired but no morning sickness), who they had told (just their parents, which made Rose feel special), and how excited and terrified she was all at once.

Michelle wasn't the first of Rose's girlfriends to have a baby. Over the past decade, most of her friends had become mothers. Then there was Daisy, who had procreated three times, all events Rose had monitored closely with a great deal of auntly interest. So although she had experienced the "I'm pregnant" announcement many times before, she still got goosebumps, and her heart beat a little faster. Every time she heard those two words, she was just as thrilled as she was the last time they had popped out of someone's mouth.

Why *was* that, Rose wondered? Her internal cynic would say, "Better her than me!" and that it was relief, not excitement, that caused the goosebumps and racing heart. The truth was, she really *was* happy when someone she cared about got pregnant, because their happiness was apparent.

After talking for an hour and a half about her pregnancy, Michelle looked at her watch and said, "Oh my God! I have to run. Shawn and I have to review some information my doctor gave me about doulas, breast pumps, and lactation consultants. I'm dying to hear how you're doing, but it'll have to wait till next time."

After Rose got home, she changed out of her work clothes and into her flannel pyjamas, then crawled into bed in a funk. Since she refused to put a TV in the bedroom and she didn't feel like reading, she moped until Jim got home from seeing a movie with a friend.

"How was your drink with Michelle?" asked Jim.

If he was expecting Rose to say "fine" and call it a night, he didn't know his wife very well. She was sure that Jim was hoping for a brief reply, but he wasn't going to get one.

"She's pregnant," Rose said with none of the enthusiasm she had shown earlier in the evening.

"Is she? Well, that's good news," Jim replied.

"Is it?" Rose asked.

"Isn't it?" Jim answered, walking down the hall to the bathroom to brush his teeth.

"Of course it is, for her," Rose hollered after him. "But I'm a little sad for me."

"Faw yoof?" said Jim, as he returned to stand in the doorway with a mouthful of toothpaste froth.

"Yes, for me," Rose said to his receding backside, which was clad in baggy boxer shorts, as he wandered back to the bathroom to rinse his mouth.

After Jim got settled in bed, he picked up a copy of *Men's Health* from the floor and started flipping through the pages. Rose wasn't about to let him off the hook that easily.

"So, about Michelle," she tried again.

"What about her?" Jim asked brusquely.

"Well, not so much about her, exactly, but maybe about me," Rose said awkwardly.

Jim looked at her quizzically. "If you're trying to say something, would you just spit it out?"

"You know. Me. And babies. Or *a* baby," Rose said, sounding even more uncertain. "I'm not sure I want one."

"That's good news, because I'm pretty sure I don't," Jim replied before returning to his magazine.

"But what if I *do* want one?" she continued.

"Do you?" Jim asked, sighing and rolling his eyes toward the ceiling.

"I might," Rose replied.

"Why don't you get back to me when you know for sure," Jim said, as though that signalled the end of their conversation.

This was going to be tougher than Rose had anticipated. "Do you think you might want a baby someday?" she persisted. "You know how good you are with Daisy's kids, and they love you to pieces."

"That's different," Jim replied. "I can give them back at the end of the day."

"But if we had one, you wouldn't *want* to give it back," Rose said encouragingly.

"I might if it talked as much as you do," Jim said, glaring at his wife.

"Babies don't talk, silly," Rose replied. "And you haven't answered the question."

"*What* question?!" Jim exploded, his patience starting to wear thin (thank God his hair wasn't, at least not yet). Rose was going to have to tread carefully.

"Whether or not you might want a baby down the road," Rose prompted.

"How should I know? I guess it's possible," Jim answered cautiously. "But I'm only just starting to feel comfortable in my job, and babies are the last thing on my mind. Honestly, Rose, I've got more important things to think about right now."

More important things?

"All right," Rose said. "I guess I can understand that. Maybe we'll talk about it again another time." Like tomorrow, she thought but didn't say. She knew when to stop.

Jim didn't respond and went back to reading an article on how to tone your abs in two hundred and forty-five easy steps. Rose swore that the guys who read *Men's Health* were just as gullible as the women who read *Cosmo*, as she reached down to pick up an old copy of that magazine from the floor beside her bed.

ை

The second baby-fever event occurred while Rose was sitting at her desk at work reviewing an article she had just written for *Dash*'s next edition. The article was a guide of prenatal resources with a sidebar on the five best exercises for pregnant women. For two weeks, Rose had been on the phone interviewing various specialists, including a doula, midwife, and labour nurse. She was totally prepared to have a baby.

Except that she wasn't having a baby.

The summer months were always the busiest time at work because the editorial team was putting together the big fall issues. As Rose was proofing her story, the editor-in-chief, Kelly MacIntosh, came into her office. At the best of times, Kelly was scattered and harried. This wasn't the best of times, however, because they were in production for the October issue, which meant tight deadlines and lots of stress.

Neither Kelly nor Rose, the most senior editors on a small staff of five, had taken a holiday that summer. Although most of the time they got along well, the strain was starting to take its toll on both of them. Kelly had come to tell Rose that she was booking the following week off, before her two young daughters went to camp.

"What?!" Rose said, louder than she should have. "We'll still be in production, and you know I can't put everything through by myself—I'll be too burnt out to see straight. In case you've forgotten, I haven't had a holiday for months either. And I've been working my butt off."

"Yes, but you don't have children, Rose," Kelly replied.

Rose's jaw dropped. She gaped at Kelly, shocked that those words had come out of her mouth. She couldn't believe that her boss had just told Rose that she didn't deserve a holiday as much as Kelly did because she didn't have kids. What drugs was she on? Or maybe her happy pills had run out, and that was her problem.

"You don't have to devalue my family unit because it doesn't include children," Rose said frostily. "Professionally speaking, I deserve a holiday every bit as much as you do." Rose was proud of herself, because in an emotional-crisis situation she usually only thought of clever comebacks the next day, when it was too late to deliver them.

Rose stomped past Kelly and down the hall to lock herself in a bathroom stall, which was the only private place a woman could have a personal meltdown at work. She decided to hold back the tears until she got home that evening and instead tried to focus on calming her breathing without hyperventilating.

As Rose inhaled and exhaled deeply through her nose, as the teacher in her yoga video instructed, she wondered if there was a human resources policy stating that employees with children couldn't insult coworkers without them, maybe some sort of emotional harassment code. She'd have to consult the staff handbook.

When Rose had composed herself enough to return to her desk, Kelly was gone. She had sent an email saying that she had an appointment for the rest of the afternoon and giving the dates she was going to be out of the office, adding that Rose could call her cellphone if there was an editorial emergency. Like what—Rose spontaneously combusted due to overwork? There was no apology, not that Rose had expected one, but in spite of that she felt a wave of disappointment wash over her. Kelly's comment had been personal, and it had stung.

Rose shook her head and sighed. It looked like she was going to have to hold the fort, whether or not she wanted to, until production was over. She guessed that life must be easier when you were the owner's daughter, as Kelly was. Rose's parents had grown and sold organic produce on a hippie commune, so she wouldn't know.

⁊

The third and most upsetting event took place as recently as three weeks ago. Rose was still recovering from it.

It began when Rose's friend Sharon delivered her first baby, a daughter. Sharon and Rose had been friends since they were five, and Sharon still lived in Wolfville. They didn't see each other much anymore, but they emailed regularly and sent birthday and Christmas cards. Sharon's was the only friendship Rose had held on to from her youth, and what she didn't know at the time was that she was about to lose it. If she had, maybe she would have handled things differently.

When Sharon got pregnant, Rose was thrilled for her and her husband, Peter. They had been trying to conceive for years, and Sharon had had several fertility treatments, so her pregnancy was a blessing. As soon as she told Rose that she was expecting, however, their relationship changed, much like it had with Michelle.

The first thing Rose noticed was that whenever she got an email from Sharon, she only talked about herself. It was all about how she was feeling, how the pregnancy was developing, the prenatal classes, the baby showers. Nothing about her work. Nothing about her hobbies. And nothing about Rose. Sharon stopped asking how Rose was doing, how Jim was, how their families were, how work was, and how her yoga was coming along. Sharon used to do all of that, but not anymore.

In the spring, Sharon had come to Toronto on business; she managed a craft shop and was attending a trade show at the convention centre. Her boss had paid for her to stay at a hotel, so she and Rose met one evening for dinner downtown. After Rose had run out of her standard list of baby-related questions and Sharon had answered them all enthusiastically, Rose had paused to take a breath. And waited.

Nothing. Not a single word had come out of Sharon's mouth. Rose couldn't believe it. *Now she'll ask me how I'm doing,* she kept thinking, as the silence grew more uncomfortable. *Now she'll ask me how Jim likes his new job,* she allowed herself to hope.

Nope. Nada.

To fill the pregnant pause, Rose had started up with more questions, only she changed the topic to Sharon's family. Finally, it was time to pay the bill and go their separate ways. As Rose got on the subway, she had a leaden feeling in the pit of her stomach that she knew had nothing to do with her overcooked steak.

On the ride home, Rose kept replaying the evening in her mind, practising what her therapist called "self-talk."

"Of course Sharon is going to be self-absorbed—she's going through a life-changing event," Rose had told herself. "You have to be understanding. You don't know what it's like to be pregnant, so you can't judge her based on what you think you would or wouldn't do if you were in her shoes. She's your friend, and you have to accept her in spite of this drastic personality change."

Did she *really* have to accept Sharon that way? Rose had come away from their dinner feeling hollow and sad, and like their friendship was dissolving.

The evening had been so upsetting that Rose hadn't discussed it with Jim, since she sensed that she wouldn't get much support considering their last conversation about babies. She thought about a couple of other friends who usually gave her good insight, but they were both mothers, and she wasn't sure they'd be able to relate to where she was coming from. So she tried to absorb it on her own, letting it simmer in her subconscious until it reached a boiling point.

After Sharon had her baby and sent Rose an email to tell her about it, the boil was so intense that the lid blew right off the pot.

Hi Rose,
This is the first free fifteen minutes I've had since Lauren was born to email a few friends. I'm exhausted but the happiest I've ever been in my whole life! I feel like a totally different person. I can't believe the silly little things I used to worry about before, like work stuff. It's all so unimportant compared to this. Now Lauren is the focus of my world. Just imagine how much you love Jim and then multiply it by a thousand. Maybe even a million! The love I feel for Lauren is exactly that, and it's the most amazing feeling in the world. I hear her waking up from her nap, so I have to go. Talk to you later.
Love, Sharon

As Rose read Sharon's email for the second time, she could feel her blood pressure rising. She couldn't believe what she had read: the "silly little things" Sharon said were insignificant were the sum total of Rose's life. Without meaning to, her friend had belittled Rose's existence.

Rose's right index finger hovered over her keyboard's "delete" button, then her hand moved back onto her lap. Her gut was telling her to erase the email and not reply—to let it go.

After all, she had been through this before. She had put distance between herself and other less close friends after they'd had babies because they no longer had much in common, and because they could never socialize with her and Jim on their own unless they wanted to fork out big bucks for babysitters, which most of the time they didn't.

Instead, Rose did something that would set off a chain of subsequent emails that took on a terrible life of their own. She messaged Sharon back.

Dear Sharon,
First of all, I'm thrilled that Lauren is healthy and the new focus of your life. I can only imagine that having a baby is such a life-changing event. I wasn't going to say anything, but I've decided to tell you that I'm going through a rough patch when it comes to babies. In a few weeks I'll turn thirty-seven, and for the first time in my life I'm torn about whether or not I want a baby. Jim isn't ready to have one now because of his new job, and as you know he's five years younger than I am, and at his age I wasn't thinking about babies either, so I can't blame him for the way he feels.

Then Rose summarized what Kelly had said to her at work that upset her so much. But she's pretty sure it was the next bit that got her into trouble.

Ever since you got pregnant, you stopped asking me how I was doing. All you talked about was your pregnancy, and I felt like you weren't interested in me anymore. I don't want to lose your friendship or intrude on your happiness, but I'm really hurt. I'm

17

not asking you to stop sending me messages about
Lauren. I'm just saying if you tacked on a "How are
you?" or a "How does Jim like his job?" at the end of
your messages, it would make a world of difference
to me. We've been friends for such a long time that I
know I can share these feelings with you.
Love, Rose

Rose had no idea what kind of a hormonal hurricane she was going to unleash when she sent that message. Two hours later, Sharon replied:

Rose, (the absence of a "Hi" or "Dear" is never a good sign)
I was shocked to receive your message. I feel like I've
been attacked, and I don't have the energy for this. I
don't want to lose your friendship, but I can't believe
how selfish you're being. This is supposed to be the
happiest time of my life, and yet all you can think
about is yourself and your feelings. You say you're
happy for me, but you can't possibly be sincere. I
think the real problem is that Jim doesn't want to
have a baby, and if that's the case and you do want
one, then I feel sorry for you.

As for asking you how you're doing, I assumed
you knew I was interested in your life and that I
didn't have to ask you specific questions. No one else
has complained about how I conduct my friendships,
so if you don't like it then I don't know where we're
supposed to go from here.
Sharon

Rose felt like throwing up. She read the email twice, to make sure she had absorbed it properly, then burst into tears. Then she deleted it so she wouldn't be able to obsess over it. Finally, without taking the time to overthink, she typed a fast response:

Hi Sharon, (Rose wasn't stooping to her level!)
Thank you for your message and for sharing your feelings with me. I'm sorry you felt attacked, because that certainly wasn't my intention. I was just trying to make you understand why I'm having a rough time, but it doesn't seem like I'm doing a good job explaining myself.

First of all, don't blame the way I'm feeling on Jim. He's part of the problem, but not all of it. There are other factors at play, including our age difference, my upcoming birthday, and, most important, my own indecision. You knew you wanted to have a baby, so you'll never understand what it's like to be unsure and to feel that time is working against you— that if you don't make a decision soon, the decision will be made for you.

Second, I can be happy for you and in personal turmoil at the same time. Emotions are complicated.

Finally, my definition of friendship is that it's interactive. I don't make my friends guess whether or not I'm interested in them. I ask them about their lives so they'll know. I don't need you to feel sorry for me. What I need is your support and empathy, and if you can't give them to me then I guess we should just leave it at that.
Love, Rose

After Rose sent that message, which she figured might be the last one ever, she emailed Jim at work and told him what had happened. As she typed, she wiped the tears from her cheeks.

Jim replied right away and said not to let Sharon's messages bother her, and that Sharon shouldn't have been so mean after Rose had gone out on an emotional limb by revealing her feelings—that Sharon was the selfish one.

When Rose needed him the most, Jim came through. Nevertheless, she still felt depressed. To cheer herself up, she did what any twenty-first-century, fast-track career woman would do: she dried her tears, blew her nose, and made an appointment to get her hair cut.

Three

ROSE ARRIVED ON TIME FOR HER APPOINTMENT, as she always did. Kaitlin, her stylist, was running late, as she always was. It was a Saturday morning, so Rose didn't mind waiting. She'd just flip through some hairstyle magazines and hope to find inspiration. At this point, her birthday was two weeks away, and if she couldn't feel good when it arrived, she wanted to at least look good.

Rose loved having her hair done, and the way Kaitlin massaged her head before washing her hair relaxed her almost into unconsciousness. When Rose's turn in the chair arrived, she knew that she was going to get the latest installment in Kaitlin's soap-operatic love life. She was a thirty-year-old punk princess, with multiple body piercings and fuchsia-and-black hair. She was tall and slender and had gorgeous green eyes. She was also smart; she could talk about politics as knowledgeably as she could discuss the benefits of auburn highlights.

For the past three years, Kaitlin had been dating a jerk on and off—more on than off, unfortunately. Every two months when Rose visited her, Kaitlin would bring her up to speed on the ongoing saga. Today the news was that she had kicked

Loser Boyfriend out again, and he had moved in with an ex-girlfriend. Kaitlin said that she'd refuse to take him back if he returned, but Rose had heard it before.

"Do you ever think you'll have a traditional relationship and family?" Rose asked her.

"Probably not," Kaitlin said matter-of-factly.

"Do you even want a family?" Rose pressed.

"I don't know," Kaitlin said thoughtfully. "I sometimes think that when I'm forty, I might adopt a seven-year-old. No one wants the older kids in foster care, and that way you beat the biological clock at the same time."

"What a good idea!" Rose said. "That never occurred to me." She had thought about adoption, of course, but only of babies. She would have to incorporate that option into her baby equation. Rose was worried, though, that an older child would arrive on their doorstep with a few bad habits—like swearing, bedwetting, and an interest in arson—so well entrenched that they'd be impossible to break.

At that point, Rose told Kaitlin about her recent baby angst and what had happened with Michelle, Kelly, and Sharon. The last story pissed Kaitlin off.

"So you're the selfish one because you aren't wrapped up in Sharon's narrow little bubble of baby happiness?" she said, her scissors snipping furiously. "Just you wait till she's fed up with changing shitty diapers, cleaning up barf, and having sore boobs from breastfeeding that she won't let her husband touch. She'll be dying for adult conversation, but she won't be able to find it because she'll emerge from her cocoon of self-absorption to find that she's driven all of her friends away."

Kaitlin didn't realize it, but Rose had just doubled her tip.

"Take Amber here," Kaitlin continued, nodding to the woman cutting hair on her left, who smiled shyly. "She's been married for years, and she and her husband have chosen not to have kids. The last thing they want to do is sit around with a bunch of self-righteous parents telling them they're missing out on the best part of life."

"Yes, but Amber *knows* she doesn't want children," Rose said sadly. "My problem is that I *don't* know, and the not knowing is making me miserable."

"Maybe you should just stop taking your birth-control pills without telling Jim," said Kaitlin conspiratorially. "I know it may seem selfish, but if you really want to get pregnant, you should think about it."

"I could never do that!" Rose replied, shocked at what Kaitlin had suggested—and at how close the sharp scissor blades were coming to her ears. "If I did, Jim would resent the hell out of both me and the baby, never mind the dishonesty issue. Besides, even if Jim was all for it, I don't think I'm ready to have a baby yet. So you see, the problem really *is* me."

At that point, Kaitlin was ready to blow-dry Rose's hair, so conversation ceased. When she was finished, Rose paid the bill, tipped her generously, made her promise not to take Loser Boyfriend back, and left smelling, looking, and feeling much better.

✑

The next morning Rose woke up, washed her hair in the shower, and then couldn't style it the way Kaitlin had. Her happy mood drooped along with her hair, and she decided that it was time to call in the big gun—Charlotte Wright, her therapist—to see if she could fit her in for a pre-birthday session. Preventive medicine, if you will.

Charlotte had a free hour on Wednesday, ten days before Rose's birthday. By a free hour Rose meant an available hour, because at nearly two hundred bucks a pop, Charlotte's time wasn't "free." And since Rose's health insurance was maxed out, she'd have to cough up the cash herself. She tried to think of it as an early birthday present to herself, although she would have preferred a Caribbean cruise or a pair of diamond earrings, neither of which you could purchase for the price of a visit with your therapist, but dream big or go home.

Charlotte's office was located above a medical clinic across from the Wellesley subway station. It was in a converted Victorian house, and Rose's family doctor was there, too. She always felt comfortable in the spacious sitting room, reading the same dog-eared copies of *National Geographic*.

At precisely quarter after four, Charlotte came downstairs to let Rose know it was her turn. Rose followed her into the cozy office, which felt like a den with its bookshelves and a claw-footed ottoman placed between two armchairs.

After Charlotte handed Rose a glass of water, Rose explained how her friends and boss had disappointed her.

Charlotte listened intently while Rose talked, occasionally scribbling on her notepad. Was she writing her grocery list, Rose wondered? Or jotting down things like "Patient is insane—recommend immediate institutionalization." When Rose finished relaying what Sharon had written in her emails, Charlotte's face got red.

"I can't stand narrow-minded, self-righteous, smug married parents!" she burst out. "I have to admit that I've been on the receiving end of those kind of comments myself."

Charlotte was tall, silver-haired, and the epitome of relaxed elegance. From the few personal details she had volunteered since Rose had started seeing her the previous year, Rose learned that she had never been married but that she had lived with a man for several years. In the end it didn't work out, but Rose didn't know why. Sometimes she got the sense that Charlotte was still wounded from the experience. She did know that Charlotte didn't have children, but she had a feeling that she would have made a great mother.

"You know, Sharon's message was very inconsiderate," Charlotte began. "She said a lot of hurtful things to you."

"Yes, she did," Rose said.

"She wasn't being a good friend," Charlotte added.

"No, she wasn't," Rose replied.

"I'm sure her hormones are all over the place right now, but even so, that's no excuse for being insensitive. From what you told me you wrote in your email, I don't think you said anything inappropriate. You were expressing your feelings with empathy and without judgment."

Rose hadn't thought that she had said anything hurtful, but it was a relief to hear a trained, objective third party say so. Even if she was paying her.

"So what am I supposed to do now?" implored Rose. "Alienate myself from my friends with babies? Because it just seems to be the ones with babies who are self-absorbed. My friends with older children seem normal by comparison."

"Babies do change people's lives dramatically, and it's a big adjustment for everyone," said Charlotte. "You could try to be more patient and lower your expectations with those friends. If you find that you're getting tired of the constant baby talk, you could pull back a bit from those friends and concentrate on other ones."

That made sense. But now it was time to discuss the bigger problem—how Rose felt about having a baby. She told Charlotte about the anxiety she was having over her indecision and Jim's indifference, and how panicked she felt about her upcoming birthday.

Charlotte smiled. "Rose, you're turning thirty-seven. That's not old in these modern times of motherhood."

"I know," Rose admitted reluctantly. "I just wish Jim knew what he wanted. I swear that one night when we first started seeing each other, he said that he *did* want a family. He doesn't remember that. What if he isn't ready to think seriously about having babies for a few more years? I don't want to become a first-time mother in my early forties, I don't think I'd have the energy. And what if, in a few years, he decides he *doesn't* want children?"

"I want to ask you one question," Charlotte said, putting down her notepad. "Are you happy?"

Clearly she wasn't happy or she wouldn't be there, Rose felt like saying. But a therapist's office is no place for sarcasm, and Charlotte didn't deserve a dose of Rose's sass. Rose might speak to her mother like that, but not to Charlotte.

Rose closed her eyes and paused before she answered. Then she opened her eyes and smiled. "You know what? Aside from the baby dilemma, I *am* happy."

"Well, that's something," replied Charlotte. "On your birthday, I want you to give yourself a blessing to counteract Sharon's email. And then if you do become unhappy—and I mean *really* unhappy—about whether or not you want a baby, come see me again."

A blessing? Rose thought, confused. She didn't belong to an organized religion. The only blessing she knew was the one her grandfather had said every year before her family ate Christmas dinner, and she could only remember half of that ("Bless us, oh Lord, and this food to our use blah blah blah..."). But she didn't think that was the kind of blessing Charlotte was talking about.

"A blessing?" Rose said. "I'm not sure what you mean."

"Tell yourself that you're fine about turning thirty-seven and you're happy with where you are in life," Charlotte replied.

"Okay, I can do that," Rose said.

"And Rose?"

"Yes?"

"Have a happy birthday."

"Thanks, Charlotte," Rose said. "I'll try."

⟡

A few days later, Rose was lying on Jim's chest in bed, pestering him as he tried to read *Men's Health,* when he made a startling announcement.

"I see two grey hairs!"

"What? Where? Pull them out and show me!" Rose cried frantically.

"You know they say if you pull out a grey hair, two more will grow back in its place," Jim said smugly.

"That's ridiculous, because I happen to know that one hair follicle only produces one hair," Rose replied. "Pull them out and give them to me. And try to be gentle."

Telling a man who is six foot two and has size fourteen feet to try to be gentle is like asking the Jolly Green Giant to tiptoe through the tulips. When Jim pulled the hairs, tears sprang into Rose's eyes.

He placed them in her palm. Sure enough, two silver hairs stared Rose in the face. Much to her relief, she discovered that she didn't mind that her rich auburn hair had a couple of white ones in the fold. It was strange, though, to know that her body was betraying her in such a noticeable way, and that she hadn't even been aware of it until Jim had pointed it out.

"See if you can find some more," Rose urged Jim, plopping herself back into position on his chest.

"You might think it's cool now, but wait till the hair on the rest of your body turns grey," said Jim, winking mischievously as he continued sifting through her head like a dad checking his child's scalp for lice.

"Don't be disgusting!" Rose said as she grabbed the magazine and swatted Jim on the head. That hadn't occurred to her. Now all she could think about was what her nether region would look like when it was snow covered.

"You're all clear, I don't see any more," said Jim.

Rose didn't think she looked old for her age. Every now and then Jim would say something that reaffirmed her self-appraisal. For example, last summer the two of them had taken the ferry from the harbourfront to Centre Island, one of the few outdoor places in the city where you could escape the humidity and smog.

On the short ferry ride, they started chatting with a friendly young woman named Keryn who was visiting from New Zealand. During the conversation, Jim went to get coffee at the snack bar, so Rose and Keryn had a chance to talk on their own about the boyfriend who was waiting for Keryn back home and whom she was debating dumping. When the ferry docked, they went their separate ways.

"She was nice," said Jim. "I wonder how old she is."

"She's twenty-eight," Rose replied. "She told me while you went for coffee."

"Twenty-eight! That's eight years younger than you!" said Jim, incredulously. "She looks older."

Rose knew that men had no idea how to accurately predict a woman's age—she actually had a hard time herself—but it didn't matter. When Jim said that, her spirit soared. It's true that Keryn did look older than Rose, probably because she had more wrinkles, likely a result of years of unprotected sun exposure on the beach.

Rose had a few wrinkles, or laugh lines as her mother liked to call them—or crow's feet as Jim liked to call them— at the corner of each eye. Her wrinkles and grey hair didn't bother her, but her cellulite did. Fortunately, that area of concern was located behind Rose's line of vision, so unless she made a concerted effort, she didn't have to see it.

Recently, there had been a contest on a morning radio show that offered as a prize ten thousand dollars' worth of cosmetic surgery. Rose often wondered whether she'd have any "enhancements" done if she won.

What the hell. Damn right she would.

Given ten thousand dollars and a talented plastic surgeon, there were things she could improve. First she'd get the surgeon to suck all of the extra fat cells out of her backside. Then she'd have a couple of moles removed, so she wouldn't have to worry about them becoming cancerous. While she wouldn't mind being a 34C instead of a 34B, she drew the line at breast enlargement because she had read too many articles about toxic leakage. With the money left over after liposuction and mole removal, she'd buy several expensive push-up bras.

From the age of eight to eighteen, Rose was seriously into gymnastics. She was so flexible, in fact, that her friends called her Rubber Band Rose. It's pretty hard to make a living as a competitive gymnast, though, and her knees started to bother her—early onset arthritis, probably—so after she graduated from high school she went to university in Toronto, where she earned a journalism degree.

Back in the old days—or more accurately, the young days—Rose had a great body. She was slender and strong. She weighed one hundred and fifteen pounds, and it was all muscle. But since she had stopped training, she'd had a hard time finding interesting ways to keep fit and stay healthy. She got bored working out at the gym, so she didn't buy a membership because it was like giving money to charity—she'd pay the fee, go once or twice, and never return. She couldn't stand aerobics classes because the instructors shouted and the music was so loud it made her eardrums vibrate. Running hurt her knees. And although she knew that swimming was the least strenuous form of exercise on the joints, she was afraid to put her head underwater. When the weather was fine she loved to power walk, and she cycled to work, but she had to put her bike away in the winter.

Over the years, among other fitness fads, Rose had tried tai chi, kick-boxing, ballet, flamenco dancing, and Pilates. Sometimes she gave them a whirl for a story she was writing for *Dash*, other times out of personal interest (could she really shake her booty like Beyoncé? Sadly, no). The only thing she had stuck with was yoga. The type she practised wasn't a vigorous cardiovascular workout, but it was good for toning muscles, overall conditioning, and stress release.

Rose thought a lot about how she should step up the amount of physical activity she did. She and Jim owned a set of hand weights, but they mostly sat in a corner of their living room gathering dust. Over the winter Rose was planning to do two nights a week of yoga videos, plus one weekly class at the fitness centre, plus two nights of weight lifting to ward off osteoporosis. On top of that regimen, she planned to power walk around their neighbourhood park when it wasn't snowing, sleeting, hailing, or any combination of the three.

These were her good intentions, at least. Rose might be a health editor, but she wasn't superwoman.

Four

ROSE COULDN'T PUT IT OFF ANY LONGER—
she was going to have to call Michelle back. This past week,
Michelle had left two messages on Rose's cellphone, which
she had ignored. It wasn't that Rose didn't like chatting with
her; she did, very much so. But the past couple of times they
had spoken, Simon had been sitting on Michelle's lap. He had
pushed the phone's keypad, making it beep in Rose's ear.

While Michelle had talked to Rose, she'd also had a
running conversation with Simon. At one point Rose told
Michelle about something that her mother said that had
upset her, and how Rose had responded maturely for a
change. Michelle had enthusiastically replied, "That's *very*
good!" Rose felt herself swell with pride under the umbrella
of her friend's encouragement—until she discovered that
Michelle was praising Simon, who apparently had just
blown the most beautiful saliva bubble in the whole wide
world.

That's when the screeching had begun—Simon, not Rose,
although she had felt like joining in. Rose thought Michelle
would cut the call short and say she'd call back later, after
she had administered a double dose of children's Gravol or

poured brandy in Simon's formula or stuck a soother in his yap to get him to shut up. But no—Michelle kept talking over Simon's cries.

"Michelle, I'm going to let you go," Rose had finally said wearily, realizing that their conversation was over.

"Really? I guess I should go, too, Shawn's coming in the door."

"I'll talk to you again soon, okay?" Rose had said, then they had hung up.

Rose hadn't had the energy to call Michelle back. She wanted to talk to her, but she was afraid that if Simon wasn't napping, or if Shawn wasn't there to take Simon from Michelle if he pulled a hissy fit, Rose would pull another Sharon, and she wasn't up for that.

This week, since Rose wasn't PMSing, she figured it was as good a time as any to dial Michelle's number. She punched the numbers on her phone, not noticing that she was holding her breath. One ring, two, three—and she had voice mail. Rose heaved a sigh of relief and left a long, friendly message. It's amazing how much catch-up news you can cram into voice mail. Now the ball was in Michelle's court. Rose wondered if she could get away with screening her calls until Simon started school.

That's when Rose remembered that Michelle was having another baby. Dammit! Why did her friends keep doing this to her?

Maybe Sharon was right: Rose *was* selfish. She was just a big baby herself. She knew that she should grow up, but she didn't know how.

The truth was, Rose missed her friends. Nothing was the same anymore, and she couldn't stop everything from changing.

⚜

Every year in the week leading up to Rose's birthday, she visited her goddaughter, Jenna. Jenna's mother, Susan, had been Rose's university roommate, and Rose had been the maid of honour at Susan's wedding. Rose and Susan weren't as close as they used to be, partly because Susan and her husband, Troy, kept moving farther into the suburbs. Last year Susan and her family had moved to a new house in Malton, which as far as Rose was concerned might as well be the moon.

The farther away Susan and Troy moved, the less often Rose and Jim visited them. Without a car, they depended on the transit system and on their friends to pick them up at the GO train station and drop them back there when they were ready to leave, because a taxi would cost a fortune. So Rose and Jim were trapped there, essentially. It seemed like it was now a once-a-year event at birthday time.

Jenna's birthday was the day before Rose's, and this year she was turning six. Susan liked to have a birthday cake for Jenna and Rose a few days before Jenna's actual birthday, when she had another cake at a children's party. Susan made and decorated both cakes herself, usually in the shape of a popular children's entertainer. This year it was Bob the Builder and Thomas the Tank Engine. The night Rose and Jim were going for dinner, they'd be carving Bob for dessert.

Susan and Troy also had a son, Jeremy, who looked like an angel with sweet blond ringlets, which he would no doubt despise and shave off when he turned thirteen, but who was in actual fact a three-year-old holy terror.

When Susan asked Rose to be Jenna's godmother, Rose was stunned. First of all, she wasn't religious. She considered herself spiritual on a certain level because she believed in some sort of a higher power, but she hadn't figured out what it was. Plus, she wasn't sure what being a godmother entailed. Would she have to teach Jenna the ways of the world? Take her for her first legal drink? Her first tattoo? There was no instruction manual for godparents—Rose had checked.

What Rose discovered was that a godmother wasn't a mentor whose role was to provide guidance throughout the various stages of her godchild's life. Instead, from what she could tell from six years of experience, a godparent was meant for one sole purpose: presents. Every birthday and Christmas, Rose had to give the goods to Jenna, who barely remembered her from one visit to the next. Plus, the kid had so much stuff already that whatever Rose took her got pushed aside to join the rest of the pile after she spent approximately five seconds checking it out.

Rose did know that Susan and Troy had made Troy's brother and his wife legally responsible for Jenna and Jeremy in the event that, God forbid, anything happened to them. Sometimes Rose thought it was a blessing that she and Jim lived in an apartment and had no worldly possessions, because their lifestyle didn't make them prime guardian material. If Rose wasn't certain she was ready to raise her own children, she'd certainly have qualms about bringing up someone else's.

On the Wednesday before Rose's birthday, she and Jim got on the GO train with gift bag in hand. Susan picked them up in her blue minivan and drove them the rest of the way. When they arrived at the house, they opened the door in time to see a wet flash of naked flesh streak past them. It was Jeremy, just out of the bath and trying to outrun Troy, who was chasing him holding a disposable diaper and a pair of Batman pyjamas.

"Hi guuyyyys!" yelled Troy as he tore down the hallway and disappeared out of sight around a corner, trying to catch his slippery charge.

Jenna, on the other hand, was ready and waiting for Rose and Jim at the door. She was wearing a pink dress with white tights and a pink-velvet headband topped off by a lacy pink bow.

It was a good thing that Jenna's a decent kid, because Rose couldn't stand pink. She particularly disliked the pink-for-girls and blue-for-boys clothing rule. It was all she could do to not back away when she saw the pink cloud of polyester moving toward her.

"That's a lovely dress," said Rose sweetly as Jenna gave her a hug.

"Thank you," Jenna said primly. "What did you bring me?"

"Jenna!" said Susan, horrified. "That's not polite. What did I tell you about saying that when people come over?"

"I'm not supposed to ask if they brought me something," said Jenna, looking down at the spotless hardwood floor, which she was scuffing with the toe of her black patent-leather shoe.

"That's okay," said Rose, gritting her teeth. "It's Jenna's birthday this week, and we *did* bring her a present."

Jenna's head snapped up so fast that Rose was worried she had given herself whiplash. Her eyes were as big as saucers.

"Can I open it?" Jenna asked excitedly.

"Sure, honey, go ahead." Jenna grabbed the gift bag out of Rose's hand and dumped it out on the floor.

One of the things Rose loved doing for kids was to buy them presents. She enjoyed wandering through the toy aisles at department stores, and the children's specialty shops were even more fun, albeit a lot more expensive. On the other end of the spectrum, at dollar stores you could buy a bag's worth of treasures for very little cash. If the child on the receiving end of the bag lost interest in its contents in a couple of days, who cared?

This year, Jenna's present had come at a yard-sale price. Literally. Although she was a devoted Bob the Builder and Thomas the Tank Engine fan, she also liked Annie the Alligator. One balmy Saturday during the summer, Rose and Jim had gone for a stroll through the park. Along the way, they had passed by a little girl who was having a yard sale on her family's front lawn. She was selling books, DVDs, stuffed animals, and an assorted array of toys.

One of them had caught Rose's eye. It was a giant talking Arnie doll, which is Annie the Alligator's pesky little brother. Rose knew that Jenna already had the matching talking Annie doll, so she was sure she'd be thrilled to get Arnie.

Rose tried to keep her cool. The girl looked like she was around ten or eleven, so Rose figured it was going to be an easy barter.

"How much for the books?" Rose asked casually.

"Fifty cents each or four for a dollar," the girl answered promptly.

"What about the DVDs?"

"A dollar each."

"And the jigsaw puzzles?"

"A dollar each."

"How much do you want for the Arnie doll?" Rose inquired nonchalantly, avoiding eye contact with both the doll and the girl as she sifted through the books.

"Ten dollars."

"Ten dollars? That's highway robbery! It's a yard sale, for crying out loud," Rose cried out loud. "I'll give you five."

"Are you kidding me?" The little girl raised an eyebrow and looked at Rose as if she had lost her mind. "It cost a hundred dollars new and it's in excellent condition. All it needs is new batteries. Ten bucks."

The scam artist! Rose wanted the doll. She looked in her wallet: all it contained was one ten-dollar bill. The kid would clean her out.

Rose knew when she was defeated. She handed over the money.

Later that week, Rose waited to watch Jenna's face light up with pleasure as she unwrapped her present. She ripped off the festive wrapping paper with wild abandon.

"Oh, it's Arnie," Jenna said matter-of-factly. "I don't watch *Annie the Alligator* anymore."

"I'm so sorry, Rose, I guess I should have brought you up to speed on what Jenna is into these days," said Susan. "She stopped watching *Annie* a couple of months ago. She even gave her Annie doll away to our next-door neighbour's daughter, who's a year younger."

Rose wasn't upset. After all, Arnie had only cost ten bucks.

"Don't worry about it," Rose replied. "It's no big deal. I should have checked with you before I bought it." She didn't offer to exchange it for something else because she was pretty sure the yard-sale girl was an "all sales final" wheeler and dealer.

"Did you bring me anything else?" asked Jenna hopefully.

"JENNA!" cried her mother, giving her daughter the hairy eyeball.

"Okay, okay, don't have a cow, man," said Jenna.

"That's it! No more *Simpsons* for you, young lady," said Susan sternly. "You're pushing it."

By that time, Troy had captured Jeremy, wrestled him to the ground, and hauled on his pyjamas. Troy came into the living room with his son neatly pinned under one arm. Two skinny little legs were whirling like an eggbeater behind him, and two tiny fists were waving wildly out in front.

"Say hi to your Auntie Rose and Uncle Jim," said Troy.

"No," said Jeremy.

"Hi, Jeremy," Rose said brightly.

"Hey, kid," said Jim.

"No," Jeremy replied.

"You don't have to say hi if you don't want to," Rose said.

"Fuck!" Jeremy shouted. "Fuck fuck fuck FUCK!"

"Guess what his new favourite word is?" said Troy, sighing. "He heard Susan say it when she banged her funny bone, and now we can't get him to stop. We've tried everything…" Troy had dark circles under his eyes and looked exhausted. "We're waiting for the call from daycare telling us he's being kicked out."

"Sorry to hear that," Rose said sympathetically. Troy put Jeremy down, and he took off running to the family room in the basement, leaving Troy to tail him so he wouldn't get into trouble. During their last visit, Troy had caught Jeremy trying to stick a butter knife into a light socket; somehow Jeremy had found a way to remove the childproof socket cover. Rose swore the boy would grow up to be an engineer or a cat burglar.

As a result of Jeremy's excess energy and mischievous nature, Rose and Jim rarely saw much of Troy during their visits. That was a shame, because he was a nice guy. He was just almost never in the same room as they were, and when he was, he couldn't carry on a conversation from start to finish without being interrupted by something Jeremy was doing that he shouldn't have been. Rose felt sorry for him. It was almost like Susan was Jenna's keeper and Troy was Jeremy's. Troy got the raw end of the deal, that's for sure.

Finally it was time for dinner: grilled steak and potatoes with carrots and peas from Susan and Troy's tiny suburban patch of a garden.

"I want to sit by Auntie Rose!" begged Jenna.

"All right, go ahead," said Susan.

Rose was setting the table. "Susan, you gave me a couple of extra steak knives," she said, handing two back.

"Really? There should be one for everyone."

"For everyone? Even the kids?"

"Yes," said Susan, stirring the pot of simmering vegetables.

Rose paused to make sure she had understood her friend correctly. Susan wanted to give a sharp knife to a three-year-old and a six-year-old? Was she kidding? Or was this a test?

"Are you sure it's safe to let the kids use them?" Rose mumbled meekly.

"Oh, sure, they'll be fine," Susan said as she waved her wooden spoon emphatically.

Troy and Jim came in from the backyard carrying the plates of steak and barbecue sauce. Jenna went over to the table, pulled out her chair, grabbed her knife, and started to say, "Guess what Auntie Rose?" while waving the knife a little too close to Rose's face for comfort.

Without thinking, Rose's right hand shot out to grab Jenna's wrist, lowering her hand and the knife down to the table in the process.

No one seemed to be paying attention, so Rose said her piece. She knew she wasn't a parent, and this wasn't her child or her house, but it was her face that was at risk of being sliced and diced.

"Jenna, sweetie, that knife is sharp," said Rose kindly. "You shouldn't wave it in someone's face, because they might get hurt."

You could have cut the silence with a knife. Jenna's face crumpled, then she pushed her chair away from the table and ran into the living room, crying.

Susan went to console her, then returned to the table.

"Jenna says you hurt her feelings," Susan said, seemingly unfazed by the incident.

"Really? I'm sorry, I didn't mean to," Rose replied. "But if Jim had waved a steak knife in my face, I would have done the same thing."

Rose looked at Jim beseechingly for support. He met Rose's gaze, then popped a piece of steak into his mouth and started slowly chewing it.

Rose wasn't going to apologize to Jenna because she didn't feel that she hadn't done anything wrong. The night was turning into a disaster. A poor excuse of a godmother Rose was, making her goddaughter cry. Rose waited for Susan or Troy to lecture Jenna about kitchen-utensil safety and respecting her elders. Rose knew that thirty-seven wasn't that old, but it was a lot older than six.

Everyone kept eating. Jenna kept crying.

After what must have been five minutes but felt like an eternity, Jenna stopped wailing and returned to the table. She sat next to her mother, across from Rose. Jeremy was sitting on Susan's lap, pinned tightly beneath her left arm. As a result, Susan was forced to eat one-handed. She couldn't cut her steak, so she picked the whole piece up with her fork and started gnawing on it like a ravenous tiger tearing apart its kill.

This was the woman who, in university, used to cringe when a cafeteria food fight broke out and who would sneak in a salad fork because the food services company didn't have them. Who needed a fork for soup and sandwiches, which were the only edible things the cafeteria served anyway?

Rose watched Jenna, who was eyeing her mother. She could have predicted what was going to happen next. In monkey-see, monkey-do fashion, Jenna stuck her fork into her steak and started gnawing on it, too.

"Jenna, would you like me to cut your steak for you?" Troy asked her.

No reply.

"Jenna, would you like to have a knife so you can cut your steak and eat it properly?" Troy tried again. That man must have the patience of Job. Rose had never seen him get ruffled, not even that time when Jeremy kneed him in the nuts.

Still no reply. Unless you count the spiteful glance that Jenna directed at Rose. How could something so small pack such a powerful emotional punch without uttering a word?

Susan kept gnawing. Maybe she was so drained from the demands of motherhood that at some point during each day, she gave up the fight and gave in to the easy way out. It might be naive for Rose to say that she'd never act like that with her own child, but it was nothing more than an educated guess, and maybe wishful thinking.

Unlike Jenna, Jeremy did want his steak knife. In fact, he was holding it in his left hand while he picked at his peas and carrots with his right and shoved them into his mouth. Rose watched as the hand holding the knife crept closer to his throat. Suddenly, the pointy tip was touching the side of his neck, dangerously near his jugular. Susan and Troy didn't notice because they were too engrossed in their dinners.

"Um, Susan? Jeremy's knife is touching his throat," Rose said, trying to keep the hysteria out of her voice as she pictured it accidentally piercing its target.

"Is it?" Susan said, glancing down at her son. "Give me that, you little scamp."

That was it? Wouldn't a slap on his hand be appropriate? Or a scolding? Was this normal twenty-first-century parenting? Rose's own parents hadn't been strict disciplinarians—they had been hippies, so relaxed when it came to rules—but she remembered stern lectures, time-outs, and occasional smacks on the hand or bum.

Rose's mother always used to say that one swift slap is effective enough to get the message across to a child who had done something wrong, and anything more was just the parents venting their frustration. Come to think of it, that might be the only sensible thing that Rose could recall her mother saying.

Somehow, while the Great Steak Knife Debate had been taking place, Jenna had turned into a ray of sunshine. She was laughing and smiling and telling a story at a hundred miles an hour about her new teacher and her swimming lessons and her ballet class and her friends at Sunday school. For a run-on sentence, it was pretty impressive.

Rose was thinking to herself, wasn't she just mad at me? Kids have the attention span of a fruit fly. Tonight, this was a good thing.

Finally, it was time for the cake. Rose had been so stressed out during dinner that she had barely eaten, so she was looking forward to dessert. So was Jenna. She came around the table to sit next to Rose as Susan brought out Bob the Builder with six flaming candles. Everyone sang happy birthday to "Auntie Rose and Jennaaaaa"—with the emphasis on Jenna, of course—then Jenna and Rose each made a wish and blew out the candles together.

It was chocolate cake, and it was delicious. And then that was it. Another birthday visit was over, another godmotherly duty done.

As Rose and Jim were putting on their coats and getting ready to leave, Jenna came over, wrapped her arms around Rose's legs, and started to cry. Troy was trying to get Jeremy to go to sleep, so Susan was going to drive them to the GO station.

"Don't go, Auntie Rose, don't go!" Jenna wailed loudly, her tears leaving wet streaks on her cheeks.

"Don't cry, Jenna," Rose said consolingly, patting her head. "Here, this is for you."

Rose bent down and slipped two folded five-dollar bills into her hand.

"Thank you," Jenna said shyly, smiling at Rose.

"You're welcome. Have a happy birthday."

"You, too," Jenna said. Then she paused and wrinkled her nose. Rose could tell that she was thinking about something. "I'm going to be six. How old are you going to be?"

"Thirty-seven."

"Wow. That's old."

"I know it is, honey. I know."

After a hug and kiss, Rose and Jim were on their way. As Susan backed out of the driveway, Rose felt relieved at having survived Jenna's tantrum, Jeremy's hyperactivity, and the range of discipline issues the evening had offered up. But she also felt something else, something strange and unsettling: an emptiness. Susan and Troy's family unit might be crazy, but it was also cozy—the kind of coziness that two people who love each other a great deal can't reproduce by themselves, no matter how hard they try.

With three days to go before her birthday, Rose could hear the clock ticking loudly. Maybe now was a good time to return to the baby equation and rework it. There was only one problem—she didn't have any new data to add to her calculations.

Five

THE REST OF THE WEEK WENT BY WITHOUT incident. At long last it was Rose's birthday. She woke up at twenty minutes after seven, just three minutes after she had been born thirty-seven years earlier. She didn't feel any different than she had the day before. She hadn't really expected that she would.

Rose looked at Jim, who was still sleeping, and thought about how lucky she was that they had each other, how lucky she was to be in good health, and how lucky she was in pretty much all aspects of her life.

That's when Rose realized that she had just given herself the birthday blessing Charlotte Wright had advised her to deliver. She had forgotten about it until that second.

Rose got up and went to the bathroom, then crawled back into bed and snuggled against Jim. He wouldn't wake up for a while, but she knew she couldn't go back to sleep. She wasn't in any hurry to move, though. They hadn't made any big plans for the day because she hadn't wanted to make a fuss. They were going to do their usual Saturday morning thing: walk to the Distillery District for brunch.

An hour later, Jim woke up. He cracked one eye open, smiled, and moved close to kiss his wife.

"Happy birthday."

"Thanks," Rose said, smiling.

"How do you feel?"

Rose paused to pinch herself. "The same as I did yesterday."

"In spite of your decrepit age, would you care for a birthday roll in the hay?"

"I just might," Rose said, her grin widening as Jim moved closer. As far as birthdays go, this one was getting off to a pretty good start. After all, weren't women in their thirties supposed to be in their sexual prime?

Eventually, they got up and showered. After Rose got dressed and before she blow-dried her hair, she turned on her computer in the office to check her emails. She had messages from several old university classmates who always remembered her birthday, and Daisy and Michelle. At some point during the day, she expected a phone call from her parents.

There was no message from Sharon. Rose hadn't expected one, but it still hurt. In more than thirty years, it was the first time that Sharon had missed her birthday. Their bond was broken.

As Rose dried her hair, she allowed herself to think about the events of the past few weeks. She had felt such anxiety about turning thirty-seven, but the morning had dawned without fanfare. What had she been expecting? Instant osteoporosis? A full head of grey hair?

What Rose had been hoping to get for her birthday hadn't yet arrived: clarity. Maybe it was coming later via FedEx. As long as it wasn't being sent cash on delivery, she'd be satisfied. But for now the mist hadn't cleared, and she realized that she still felt the same way about whether or not she wanted to have a baby. Unsure.

When Rose turned off the blow-dryer, she also consciously switched off the part of her brain that controlled baby-related thoughts. She decided not to worry about babies anymore today. After all, this was *her* day. Tomorrow she would start fretting again.

The late-autumn morning was sunny and warm. Rose loved this time of year. She and Jim set off for the Distillery District. As they walked briskly hand in hand, she took a deep breath and exhaled slowly, savouring her first few hours as a thirty-seven-year-old.

Back at home after brunch, Rose and Jim decided to watch a movie on Netflix. Before they started, Rose checked her phone messages; there was one from her mother, another from Daisy and Jim's parents. While she was in the bedroom changing into yoga clothes, Jim was lighting the candles on a chocolate-mousse cake he had bought the night before at a bakery and had hidden at the back of the fridge.

When Rose walked into the living room, her husband sang happy birthday, a little off-key but charming just the same, while the candles flickered: three on one side, seven on the other. She closed her eyes, made a wish, opened her eyes, and blew. All of them went out.

"What did you wish for?" Jim asked.

"You know I can't tell you that," Rose replied. "If I do, it won't come true."

"You can tell me—I'm your husband. You're supposed to tell me everything."

"Everything except birthday wishes," Rose said, giving Jim a hug and a kiss on the lips.

The truth was, Rose didn't want Jim to know what she had wished for: baby-related clarity.

When they went to bed that night, Rose was full of tea and cake and flushed with happiness. She had survived turning thirty-seven. She was surprised at how relieved she was that the day was over. She had been putting a lot of pressure on herself to have a big baby revelation, and when it didn't happen and her world didn't crumble, it felt like a weight had lifted.

⟳

On Monday, Rose got the shock of her life—she discovered that she had missed a birth-control pill, but she couldn't figure out when. What with having dinner at Susan's, being busy at work, worrying about her birthday, and being consumed with baby anxiety, she had forgotten to take a pill.

Good Lord. Could she be pregnant?

Thankfully, Rose had been planning to work at home that day. Jim had already left for work, so she threw on jeans and a turtleneck, grabbed her wallet and keys, ran downstairs and dashed across the street to the pharmacy. When she got there, she tossed three pregnancy tests into the basket, then threw in paper towels, a chocolate bar, and a pack of gum as decoys.

When Rose pulled out her credit card to pay, she made sure that her wedding band and engagement ring were in plain sight. For some reason, whenever she bought a pregnancy test she was always afraid the cashier was going to look at her, wink, and say loudly, "Pregnant, are we? Is that good or bad news?" After which Rose would turn an embarrassing shade of red before the floor opened up and swallowed her.

If that happened right now, Rose didn't know what she'd tell the cashier. Would it be good or bad news? She was so flustered, she had no idea. Luckily, the only question the cashier asked was whether she had her in-store rewards card.

As soon as Rose got home, she ran to the bathroom, ripped open the first box, and grabbed the plastic wand. *Dammit!* She didn't have to pee. She ran back to the kitchen, filled a large glass with water, and downed it. Then she raced back to the bathroom.

47

Rose sat on the toilet and waited. Nothing. Not a dribble. She stretched to the right and turned on the sink faucet. Still nothing. She stretched to the left and turned on the bathtub tap. As water gushed on either side of her, she closed her eyes and visualized the cascading waves at Niagara Falls.

That worked, and Rose sprang into action. After the task was complete, all she had to do was wait for one minute, then she'd know her fate. She still wasn't prepared to consider the consequences if the test was positive.

That minute was the longest sixty seconds of her life.

Rose had experienced false alarms before, but this didn't feel the same. Up until now, she had always been relieved when the result was negative. Would today be different?

Rose was about to find out in three seconds. Two. One. She was afraid to look, but she forced herself to squint at the two white windows in the wand, which by now had coloured stripes in them.

One blue stripe in each window, in fact. *Shit!* She couldn't remember what that meant. Did that mean she was pregnant or not pregnant? What had she done with the pamphlet that had come with the test? Not all brands of tests record their results the same way, so it was easy to get them mixed up.

After a frantic search, Rose found the box in the pharmacy bag in the bathroom garbage can, where she had hastily thrown it. She scanned the steps quickly. There it was: a blue stripe in the first box and no stripe in the second box meant she wasn't pregnant.

Rose read on. A blue stripe in both boxes meant she was likely going to have a baby in roughly nine months or forty weeks, whichever came first.

Rose sat down abruptly on the bathroom floor. Now she could let herself analyze how she was feeling. So, how *was* she feeling?

Nauseous, for sure (was it too early for morning sickness?). And stunned. And scared. And maybe—just maybe—relieved. And excited. After all, if she *was* pregnant, the indecision that had been messing with her mind the past few weeks would be gone. A higher power—well, two higher powers, a studly sperm and a seductive egg—would have decided for her. If that were the case, she could finally put her baby calculations to bed.

If Rose was pregnant, it wouldn't be the end of the world, she reassured herself. Sure, the timing wasn't great, but neither was it a disaster. She and Jim would focus on the positives and manage somehow.

Shit! Rose had forgotten entirely about the other half of the "we" in the equation. You know, the unwitting sperm donor—her husband. He was going to flip out when she told him. Her heart sank. How could she be happy about having a baby if he wasn't? Because she was certain she could be happy.

Rose decided that it was time to put Plans B and C into action. She went back to the kitchen and tossed back three more glasses of water as fast as tequila shots. She was going to take the second and third tests. If they were all positive, she would call her doctor and make an appointment to take one at her office to be absolutely certain.

After more tap turning and water gushing, Rose completed the tests. They were both negative. When she looked at the first test again, she realized that the blue line was faint. Maybe that test had been defective. Or maybe she had willed herself to see the second blue line.

Rose was surprised to discover that she felt more disappointed than relieved. When she thought she was pregnant, it was like being lifted from the quicksand of indecision in which she had been mired for so long.

As Rose was still worried about the one potentially positive test, she dialled the office number of Jean Davies, her doctor. After being put on hold for almost ten minutes, Dr. Davies's reassuring voice came on the line. When Rose explained what had happened, Dr. Davies told her to relax. Then she said that if two out of three pregnancy tests said she wasn't pregnant, she probably wasn't pregnant.

Because Rose didn't know when she had missed a pill, Dr. Davies told her to stop taking the rest of them and wait a whole cycle before starting a new package. And if Rose continued to worry that she might be pregnant, or if she didn't get her period while she was off the pill, she should make an appointment to have a test done at her office.

Rose felt better after she hung up, but now she had a decision to make. Should she tell Jim what she had just gone through? She wanted to, but after much internal debate she decided against it. What was the point? What would she say? "Honey, guess what? For a few minutes today I thought I was pregnant, but it turns out I'm not. I'm relieved *and* disappointed. I can't tell which emotion is stronger, which means I'm just as confused about whether I want a baby. Now would you be a sweetheart and please pass the pepper?"

Rose would have to tell Jim that she was taking another "pill break" for a month to give her reproductive system a rest. He shouldn't be suspicious because she had done it a couple of times before. They would have to use an alternative contraceptive, which neither of them enjoyed. When Rose went off the pill their sex life suffered, because Jim was worried he'd knock her up—although, clearly, not worried enough to abstain. And as everyone except teenagers knows, the best form of contraception is abstinence.

Four weeks. They'd have to make the best of it.

Six

EVERY MORNING WHILE ROSE ATE HER CEREAL, she read her horoscope in *The Star*. Sometimes it was spookily accurate, while at other times it wasn't even close. She took it with a grain of salt and enjoyed it for its entertainment value. On the Thursday after her birthday, here's what it said:

> *This is the kind of day when your worst suspicions about yourself seem to be confirmed. But this is just negative thinking. You are not as old, fat, broke, selfish, ugly, uptight, and stupid as you fear. You're just as great as you were last week.*

Rose wasn't sure if that was supposed to make her feel better or worse about aging. Before she read her horoscope, she wasn't feeling fat, ugly, or stupid—old, selfish, and uptight, maybe, and she always felt broke—but now she was having second thoughts about the first three.

Rose admitted to herself that she did have days when she felt fat, ugly, and stupid. Didn't everyone? She was old enough to know that she wasn't the only woman to have moments of self-loathing. There were times when she couldn't stand her hair, her hips, her hangnails, or her hemorrhoids (which hadn't flared up in months, touch wood). Put it this way: if she passed a mirror when she was feeling less than enthusiastic about herself, she'd look the other way. But once in a blue moon, everything would come together: she'd have a good hair day, spotless skin, a manicure, and a new outfit. She'd feel confident and attractive.

Then her mother would call, and that self-confidence would disappear into thin air like Amelia Earhart.

Rose loved what she did for a living. Not that her job couldn't be stressful, frustrating, and tedious at times, but for the most part being a health editor made her happy. She enjoyed helping writers craft health, fitness, and well-being articles that were relevant to women, and writing the occasional story herself.

Rose had started working at *Dash* seven years ago, and it had stuck like false eyelashes on a beauty queen. She earned a decent, if not an extravagant, salary. She got four weeks of annual paid vacation and her teeth cleaned twice a year for free. When deadline tension caused her shoulders to creep up until they touched the bottom of her earlobes, she could go for a therapeutic massage. She was sent an endless supply of health products from companies that hoped to get mentioned in the magazine, from PMS-fighting tea to eucalyptus-scented eye pillows. She'd had worse jobs, all right.

Rose worked with an eclectic group of women. It was a small staff: there was Kelly MacIntosh, the editor; Alison Turner, the art director; Rima Kumar, the editorial assistant; Yuki Miyagi, the art department assistant; and Rose. They were like the United Nations: Kelly's grandparents had immigrated from Scotland; Alison was from Australia; Rima's parents had come over from India; and Yuki and her family had moved from Japan when she was three. Rose liked to joke that she was a direct descendant of Nova Scotia hippies.

There were no men at their office apart from a couple of sexist louts in the sales department whom the editorial team did their best to avoid. The women were devoted to their jobs and tried hard to forgo office politics and in-fighting. Like all close relationships, however, some days ran more smoothly than others, depending on the amount of estrogen in the atmosphere.

Occasionally Rose daydreamed about launching a free-lance career. She was super organized, so she was confident that she'd be disciplined enough to be her own boss. Plus, it would be nice to have more professional freedom and the chance to write about more than how to battle varicose veins and still stay fit. But because of Jim's career change, her free-lance aspirations would have to wait.

The *Dash* team was divided into those who had children, those who didn't, and those who wanted them. Kelly was forty-one and married to a successful divorce lawyer; they had two daughters, Grace and Eileen, ages nine and five, respectively, who attended an expensive private girls' school. Alison was thirty-eight and married to a landscaper; they had two sets of identical twins, four-year-old Jack and Robert and seven-year-old Emma and Sara. Yuki was twenty-three and thoroughly enjoying being single. Rima was twenty-seven and had agreed to participate in a "modern" arranged mar-riage orchestrated by her parents, which meant that she and her fiancé would meet and, if sparks flew, proceed with the engagement. If they didn't, they'd politely shake hands and go their separate ways.

For the time being, Rima was "engaged" to a thirty-six-year-old accountant from Jaipur who was travelling with his parents over the holidays to meet her. She couldn't wait to have children and constantly chattered about impending motherhood. Yuki, on the other hand, was a going concern—

her idea of commitment was a one-night stand where, instead of sneaking out of the guy's bedroom at five o'clock in the morning to hightail it home without saying goodbye, she stayed for a Pop-Tart. Children? Not even a blip on her radar.

Alison always looked tired. When she described a typical workday morning in her house, Rose was dumbfounded. It went like this: up at six; grab a quick shower before the kids wake up (it had been years since she'd had time to soak in the tub or blow-dry her long hair, which she stubbornly refused to cut); make lunches for the kids to take to school; compile a list of that day's reminders for the babysitter, who picked the kids up after school and looked after them until Alison and her husband got home from work; down a glass of orange juice fortified with calcium (Rose's influence); shove a granola bar in her mouth (toast takes too long and cereal goes soggy); pile the kids into the minivan; shuttle them to school; then drive to work. All by nine o'clock. Three hours of complete and utter chaos.

When Rose listened to Alison describe those mornings, she was amazed. Sure, her husband helped, but like in most traditional families, mother is the glue.

One morning, Alison arrived at work half an hour late looking especially frazzled.

"What happened to you?" Rose asked.

"Don't ask," Alison replied. "You don't want to know."

"I do, actually," Rose said, grinning. "It'll probably be an entertaining story."

Alison shot Rose a dirty look. "Well, first of all, our hot water is on the blink so I couldn't take a shower. That always puts me in a bad mood, because it's the only thing that helps me wake up. Then Jack and Emma said they were itchy. So I checked both of them and they've got chicken pox. It's going around their school, so it's only a matter of time till the other two get it. After I had calmed them down—they went berserk when they saw the spots—I had to find the calamine lotion and swab them from head to toe. Then I had to get Derek to stay home from work so he could take them to the doctor while I drove Sara and Robert to school."

Alison glanced at the clock. "And only half an hour late. Not bad."

"You poor thing," Rose said sympathetically. "I don't think I'd be able to handle something like that so early. I don't wake up fully before eight."

"Yeah, well, neither do I," Alison said dryly. "In fact, I've always hated getting up early, and it's something I haven't gotten used to. Personally, I think six o'clock is an obscene hour for sane people to get up, never mind having to trip over four rug rats who are constantly underfoot. Sometimes I want to scream 'Shut up, everyone!' How guilty do you think *that* makes me feel?"

Rose had confided in Alison about how conflicted she was about having a baby, and to her surprise and delight, Alison had been really supportive. So when Rose looked her in the eye and said, "Maybe I don't think I want kids after all," Alison replied, "No, you don't," shaking her head slowly from side to side.

Then Alison smiled, and Rose saw a twinkle in her eyes. That's the part that got her. Because she knew that no matter what kind of grief Alison's kids gave her, or how much she hated getting up early to cater to their needs, she loved them. And she'd rather have a crazy, sleep-deprived life with them than a calm, restful one without them.

Would Rose feel the same way if she were a mother? That was the million-dollar question.

❧

Rima had been getting on Rose's nerves. She was sweet, as smart as a Mensa member, and a hard worker, but all she had been talking about for a month—ever since the arranged-marriage deal went down—was how excited she was about her potential nuptials and how she couldn't wait to have children.

One afternoon, Rima came into Rose's office, stood next to the desk, and pulled her shirt away from her stomach.

"Sometime next year this is going to be me, Rose!" Rima said excitedly. "I can't *wait* to be pregnant."

Rose had a sudden urge to slap Rima. Instead, with what she hoped was a hint of saccharine, she said, "That's nice, but don't you think you're jumping the gun? After all, you haven't even met what's-his-name yet."

"It's Madangopal, and you know it," said Rima petulantly. "I've told you at least a dozen times."

Oh, at *least* a dozen times, Rose groaned inwardly. But she kept her mouth closed, which was a massive accomplishment considering that she was PMSing.

Every now and then Rose and Rima would be discussing some inane topic, such as Rose's aversion to needles or how the sight of blood made her squirm. Rima would take those opportunities to say, "If you feel like that, Rose, you'd better not have children."

The urge to smack Rima when she made those comments was strong, but Rose was pretty sure that *Dash*'s HR department would frown upon the physical abuse of junior staff members, no matter how annoying they were. So instead she sat on her hands and counted to ten thousand. Slowly.

The truth is, Rose was offended when Rima told her that she'd better not have children. Just because certain things made Rose squeamish didn't mean she wasn't cut out to be a mother. Rose felt like Rima was judging her by her own good-parenting yardstick and condemning Rose to a lifetime of childlessness. If anyone was going to make that decision, it was going to be Rose, on her own terms and in her own time.

Come to think of it, Rose couldn't stand the word *childless*. Instead, she preferred to say that she "didn't have children." *Childless* had such a finality about it and a negative connotation—like the reason she didn't have children was because she was barren (there was another nasty word, right up there with sterile) or selfish. Alison's theory was that Rose didn't like *childless* because she was in emotional conflict, but Rose didn't agree. Even if she eventually chose not to have a baby, she was pretty sure she'd still think the word stunk.

What did Rima think she knew about Rose or her potential ability to parent that would prompt her to make such inflammatory statements? Besides, Rima could end up being a pushy soccer mom who embarrassed her shy child by screaming at the coach when he refused to put her kid in the game. No one knows what kind of parent they're going to be until they become one, not even Rima.

Rose knew she shouldn't let Rima push her buttons. After all, Rima was the kind of traditional woman who was planning to take her husband's last name when she got married, arguing that she wouldn't feel like they were a "proper family" otherwise. When she dropped that hot potato into Rose's lap one day, Rose pointed out defensively that she and Jim had different last names, so did that mean Rima didn't think they were a proper family? Rose knew she had backed her into corner, and a crimson flush spread over Rima's face.

"Well, um, no, of course not, Rose," Rima stammered. "I believe that you and Jim *feel* as though you're just as much a family as if you had the same last name." That's what Rima said, but Rose knew she didn't believe it.

When Rima spouted that Stepford wife mumbo-jumbo, Rose wanted to boot her butt into the twenty-first century. Rose had to admit that she felt much the same way about a wife taking a husband's last name as she did about abortions that are used as birth control: she was pro-choice, but she could never do either herself, and she always felt a twinge of disappointment and disrespect for the women who did. That may be a quasi-feminist assessment, but it was an honest one.

Mad Max's last name was Gopalakrishnan. Rima's was Kumar. Feminist principles aside, Rose thought that Rima would be better off sticking with her two-syllable surname.

When Rose and Jim got married, he told his parents that Rose was keeping her last name for career purposes. That's not why Rose didn't exchange Ainsworth for Mercer, but if it's what Jim chose to tell himself and others so he didn't feel like she was rejecting either him or some old-fashioned custom that he accepted, she could live with that.

Rose and Rima came from different cultures, which is partly why Rose bit her lip when Rima said something that raised her feminist hackles. She was in no position to judge Rima's beliefs or decisions, even if she didn't agree with them. The other reason Rose kept quiet was that they had to work together, and thus see each other almost every day. Just like in a marriage, she was discovering, it was important to pick your battles with your colleagues wisely.

⌘

As far as bosses go, Kelly wasn't bad. She respected Rose's editing abilities and, most of the time, let her do her own thing. She was often occupied outside the office, attending industry events and promoting the magazine to potential advertisers. Rose didn't mind spending most of her time in the office because she considered herself one of the "worker bees" and didn't enjoy schmoozing.

Dash didn't have a managing editor, so Rose was responsible for assigning and tracking stories, as well as editing them. Health was her main area of expertise, but she ended up working on all of the articles to a certain degree, depending on Kelly's schedule and how much she was around to lighten the load. Rima helped with the administrative paperwork and some of the smaller writing and editing assignments.

In addition to being Married To Money (Anthony Lawson III, a divorce lawyer with a booming practice), Kelly also Came From Money. In the 1970s her mother, Nancy, inherited a bundle when *her* father, a wealthy investment banker and committed chain-smoker, died of lung cancer at the age of sixty.

Nancy was only twenty-three. An only child—her mother had been killed in a car accident when Nancy was a teenager—she was the sole heir to her father's fortune. At that time, she was still intent on pursuing a track and field career, but when she snapped her right Achilles tendon three years later, she took a chunk of her inheritance money and launched *Dash*. At thirty she married David MacIntosh, the magazine's publisher; she had Kelly when she was thirty-six and a son, Thomas, at thirty-eight. With the help of a nanny, cleaning lady, and cook, she continued to work full-time. When it came to career chutzpah, *Cosmo*'s Helen Gurley Brown had nothing on Nancy.

Ten years ago, Kelly joined the magazine as associate editor, eventually replacing Nancy when she resigned her editorship to become the CEO of the Cancer Society. That was shortly before Rose joined *Dash*. When Rose started working at the magazine, Kelly's daughter Grace was just two years old; Eileen came along two years later. When her boss's second daughter was born, Rose assumed that Kelly would start leaving the office earlier at night and cutting down on her events schedule. She was wrong. Instead, Kelly arranged for Grace's babysitter, Juanita, to move into her mansion and take on full-time nanny duties.

Rose was surprised and disheartened. She would have thought that a woman whose own mother had been orphaned so young would have put the sanctity of family ahead of career ambitions. Kelly loved her girls, no question, and Rose knew that she always felt torn about the time she spent away from them. But Kelly had been raised by two workaholics, and she had married a workaholic. That was the only world she knew.

One evening, when Kelly and Rose were both waiting for the elevator at six-thirty, Rose asked what Kelly had planned for dinner. It was still rush hour, so she had a half-hour commute ahead of her in her sleek silver Saab, which meant she wouldn't pull into her four-car garage until close to seven.

"I don't know," Kelly sighed, pulling her Kate Spade purse higher up her shoulder. "I might grill some salmon if I can muster up the energy. Anthony's usually pretty good at helping with dinner, if he gets home on time."

On time. Since when was seven considered "on time"? Rose had grown up eating dinner at five o'clock sharp, when all four Ainsworths had sat down at the oval mahogany dining-room table to eat an organic recipe that John and Joanne had created together. It was family time.

Rose usually got home at around six, but it was production week so tonight she had stayed a little longer. Jim would have gotten home at five-thirty, and when Rose crossed the threshold of their apartment, she would be greeted by the smells of supper simmering. The table would be set, and after

Rose had hung up her coat, changed into her comfy clothes, and washed her hands, her husband would serve what he had cooked. On weekend nights, Rose took over. Their rule was that whoever didn't cook had to wash the dishes.

There was a comfort in routinely eating meals with your loved ones. Other working moms Rose knew shut off their computers at five on the dot and raced home to shove something on the stove or in the oven. If Kelly had wanted to, Rose often thought, she could do that, too.

"What about the girls? Won't they be starving by then?" Rose asked.

Kelly looked at her sheepishly. "Anthony and I don't eat with the girls during the week. Juanita fixes something for them before we get home. She's a much better cook than I am," she added almost apologetically.

"Oh," Rose replied, with what she hoped came across as an air of interested indifference. The wave of sadness that rippled through her body caught her off balance, as she pictured Grace and Eileen eating a nutritious meal of beef burritos—Juanita was a Mexican immigrant in her mid-fifties and fiercely protective of the MacIntosh girls—with their eyes darting frequently to the kitchen clock, never knowing for certain when their mother or father would walk through the door but always hoping it would be sooner rather than later.

Once, when Kelly was having an attack of working-mother guilt, which always occurred after returning from an out-of-town business trip, she confessed that when Eileen had started to talk, she would call both Kelly *and* Juanita "Mama." Rose's heart bled when she heard that, and she had to turn away so Kelly wouldn't see two tears that trickled out—one for Grace, who was old enough to know which woman was her mother and ache for her when she wasn't near, and one for Eileen, who was not.

Since "workaholic" wasn't listed on Rose's resumé—she'd bust her butt eight to nine hours a day but claimed the time that followed as personal—she made a mental promise to herself: if she ever had children, she'd make sure they knew their mother.

Seven

YUKI WAS A TONIC. SHE WAS YOUNG ENOUGH NOT to have any of the weightier worries that plagued Rose, Kelly, Alison, and Rima—in a word, children. For example, Kelly worried that she wasn't devoting enough time to her daughters because she was consumed with her career, Alison fretted that her professional life was suffering because she put the twins and her husband first, Rima wasn't able to enjoy the present because she was desperate to conceive, and Rose was giving herself an ulcer wondering if motherhood was for her.

Every Monday, Rose couldn't wait for Yuki to drag herself into the office, rumpled and reeking of cigarette smoke from whatever all-night rave she had been to over the weekend, still mildly hungover and yet showing up to work on time. Yuki was Alison's organizational right hand in the art department, and even though this was her first magazine job, she could keep up with the rest of them. Rose could say this for Kelly: she didn't fool around when she was hiring staff.

The previous night, Yuki had stayed out dancing till three in the morning at an underground club. Rose smiled fondly at her description of the sticky dance floor covered in spilled booze, the wonky sound system, and the three phone numbers that Yuki had come home with.

"Rose, you would *not* believe this one guy," Yuki said, rolling her eyes toward the ceiling. "He's going out with this girl I know—I mean we're not friends, but she knows another friend of mine—and he came right up to me while the girl was in the bathroom and asked me out. I mean, come *on*! Did he think I was going to say yes?"

"Did you?" Rose asked, curious.

"What do you think?" said Yuki.

"Was he cute?"

"Yeah, *really* cute."

"Then I think that, in spite of his ravishing good looks, you took the high road and, out of respect for the sanctity of the sisterhood of women, you turned him down," said Rose.

"What drugs are you on? Oh, right, I forgot, you don't *do* drugs, you big square," said Yuki, laughing. "And your parents were hippies. That's so sad! Anyway, of course I said I'd go out with him. It's not like he's married to that girl. They're just dating."

Rose couldn't help but laugh. She and Yuki didn't share a moral compass, but that's partly why Rose liked her so much. Yuki was young and carefree, and her biggest worry was whether her rent cheque would bounce before she got her next paycheque. She thrived on living in the moment, as she should at her age.

"Anyway, that was my bizarro weekend. How was yours?" Yuki asked.

"It was okay, we didn't do anything special," replied Rose. "I've been having a weird bout of insomnia lately, so I didn't get much sleep."

"Well, you're the health editor. Wave your magic wand and make it disappear," Yuki said.

"Very funny. Don't you have work to do?"

"Yeah, I suppose so. Better get at it. See you later." Yuki flapped her hand at Rose as she sauntered away, teetering on her platform heels.

After Yuki left, Rose decided to call Dr. Davies to see if she could squeeze in an appointment later in the day. Rose had never suffered from insomnia before, and she was concerned. Dr. Davies had a cancellation at twelve-thirty, so after Rose ate a ham-and-cheese bagel she walked from her building at Bay and College to the doctor's office on Wellesley. When she arrived, she checked in with the receptionist, took a seat, and picked a magazine off the table.

While Rose was flipping through the pages, a young woman came into the waiting room with a baby strapped to her chest and a little boy in tow who must have been two or three. After she checked in, the woman sat a couple of seats from Rose. She unwrapped her child from the sling and put him—or her, it's hard to tell when they're bald and not wearing pink or blue—on her lap, cradling the infant's wobbly head in her cupped hands. She cooed at her child, but not in that irritating way that some people reserve for infants or pets. This was just a gentle, quiet murmur.

The woman, who looked about ten years younger than Rose, seemed to wear motherhood as comfortably as a soft old sweater. The older child amused himself by crawling back and forth under the chairs, singing quietly. Rose stared at the baby, who couldn't have been any more than a few weeks old and whose gaze was locked on its mother's.

Suddenly Rose saw the baby smile at its mom. Her chest tightened, and a strange warmth flooded her body, as though her temperature had risen by a few degrees. Was this what motherhood felt like: this warm, full-body sensation? Was Rose's heart trying to tell her something?

Then the little boy—who was still crawling on his hands and knees under the chairs—kicked Rose in the leg, and her maternal yearning disappeared like a deadbeat dad's child-support cheques.

Whew, close call. That feeling must have been a hot flash. Maybe Rose was perimenopausal. She'd ask Dr. Davies about it.

Rose turned her attention back to the magazine. The following headline caught her eye: "The Childless Revolution." It was a short article, and Rose read it quickly. Basically, the theme was that more women are finding life without children fulfilling, which marks a historic shift in a society that has traditionally been based on family values. The article divided women without children into three categories: (1) those who are positively child-free; (2) those who are religiously child-free; and (3) those who are environmentally child-free.

The first category consisted of women who knew they didn't want children. Rose didn't fall into that group. The second, from what she could tell, was made up solely of Catholic nuns. And the third was women who didn't want to contribute to what they believe is an already overpopulated planet. Rose agreed that the world is overpopulated, but that knowledge wouldn't stop her from having a baby.

The writer had left out a fourth category: Rose's. It consisted of women who were riddled with indecision.

The article was interesting because it only described the benefits of not having children, including the chance for women to develop their careers fully, an enhanced intimacy with their mates, the lack of financial, emotional, and time pressures, and the freedom from fear of being a bad mother or having a difficult child. If Rose had to pick one major advantage of not having kids, it would be the last one. The rest, Rose was pretty sure she could cope with.

Probably every mother Rose knew would agree with that list, but then they'd be quick to point out the rewards of having children. And each of them would say the same thing: "When you put your children to bed at night and they wrap their arms around your neck and say they love you, nothing else compares."

That's it? That's the ultimate reward? A warm, fuzzy feeling? It sounded too simple. On the other hand, Rose knew how great it felt when Ella, Katie, and Ryan hugged her and told her they loved her. If they were her kids instead of Daisy's, maybe she'd understand how much more powerful those gestures and words could be. As everyone kept saying, "It's different when they're your own."

That's what everyone said. But what if it wasn't true for her?

As Rose finished the article, Dr. Davies appeared and ushered her into her office.

"What can I do for you today?" she asked, scanning Rose's file.

"I've been having occasional bouts of insomnia, and I wondered whether I should take an over-the-counter sleeping pill...or something stronger."

"Has this happened before?" Dr. Davies peered at Rose curiously, as though she were studying an interesting specimen under a microscope.

"No, that's why I'm concerned."

"How's your diet?"

"Fine. You know I eat well, except for my chocolate habit."

"Are you exercising regularly?"

"Yes, I'm still walking or biking to work and I'm doing yoga at home a couple times a week. I'm going to sign up for a class over the winter."

"That's good." Dr. Davies glanced down at Rose's chart, then peered over her glasses. "Are you working hard?"

"No harder than usual, I guess."

"Rose, when was the last time you and Jim took some time off?"

Rose furrowed her brow and bit her lip as she tried to remember.

"You know, it isn't a good sign if you can't remember your last holiday."

"I know, I'm thinking. I know we haven't taken one since before Jim started his new job, and that was...let me see... thirteen...no, fourteen months ago."

"Young lady," Dr. Davies said sternly, "your problem is that you need a vacation."

"I know," Rose sighed heavily. "But we're always trying to save money to buy a house or airfare to visit our families. There's never enough money on top of that for a getaway for just the two of us."

"Then maybe you had better think about skipping a trip to see your families for a year, and instead take a proper vacation. Right now you're burnt out and your body has gone into overdrive, which is why you aren't sleeping. You should listen to what it's trying to tell you."

Dr. Davies picked up a yellow notepad and a pen. "In the meantime, I'm going to write you a prescription for a new sleeping pill that's non-addictive and won't dehydrate you like some of the older ones on the market. I'm only going to give you ten to see if they agree with you, and you can cut them in half at first until you get used to them. Oh, and stay away from chocolate and anything else containing caffeine or alcohol after dinner."

"I will," Rose said meekly. She hated lying to her doctor, but give up chocolate? She had to be kidding. Rose didn't smoke or do drugs, she rarely drank alcohol, coffee had never touched her lips, and she was in a monogamous relationship.

Chocolate was her only vice, if you could even call it that. Dr. Davies might as well have told her to go home, eat a nutritious, well-balanced meal, do yoga, chop off her right arm, and try to have a good night's sleep.

Well, fine. Rose would give up her after-dinner chocolate habit. That just meant doubling her intake during the day.

Dr. Davies scribbled something illegible on her prescription pad, tore off the page, and handed it to Rose. It wasn't until Rose started walking back to the office that she realized she had forgotten to ask her about the hot flash.

⚭

When Rose returned to the office, there was an email from Kelly in her inbox.

> *Dear Dash editorial staffers,*
> *In an effort to promote an environment of wellness in the workplace, and in recognition of our hectic schedules, I'd like to propose bringing in a yoga instructor to the office on Tuesdays and Thursdays at lunchtime. There will be a fee for her services, but it will be minimal because of the group rate. If you're interested, please reply to this message no later than noon on Friday.*
> *Best, Kelly*

Great! Rose had been planning to take a yoga class this winter anyway, and now she could squeeze in two classes a week during the workday, which meant she wouldn't have to trek through any nasty weather getting to and from her local fitness centre in the evening. Plus, it would be cheaper.

Rose emailed Kelly to tell her to sign her up. At the end of the day, another email went around:

Dear Dashers, I had no idea how much stretching and relaxation you all needed! Thanks for everyone's enthusiastic and prompt responses. Our first yoga class (yes, I'm coming too!) will be this Thursday at 12:30 p.m. Wear comfortable clothes, and if you have a mat, bring it (if you don't, you can buy one from Teena, our teacher).
See you there! Cheers, Kelly

That night, while Jim was at the gym, Rose put on her yoga clothes and took out one of her yoga DVDs. As she put her taut muscles through their paces, she realized just how long ago it was that she was a limber gymnast. A couple of nights of at-home yoga wasn't enough to loosen the grapefruit-sized knots in her shoulders as she pushed her bum upward into downward dog pose, then flattened into spine-lengthening cobra pose. When Rose relaxed into child's pose, she inhaled and exhaled deeply.

By the time Thursday arrived, after two nights of stretching and strengthening at home, Rose's muscles were sore but she was confident she could get through the class without embarrassing herself. Besides, Yuki and Rima, who were both younger, had never done yoga. The beginner-level pace would suit Rose fine.

Ten minutes before class was scheduled to begin, the five of them trooped into the biggest boardroom in the office and waited for Teena to arrive. Five minutes later, a middle-aged woman with short, dark hair and an ample spare tire walked through the door, an orange mat tucked under her left arm.

"Hi there!" she chirped brightly. "I'm Teena, your yoga instructor. Is this everyone?"

"It is," said Kelly. "We're all here." But even she couldn't quite hide a twinge of surprise that their teacher resembled a human teddy bear.

Rose decided that it didn't matter what Teena looked like. The important thing was whether she could whip them into shape and melt away their stress.

With an experienced flick of both wrists, Teena rolled her mat out onto the floor and sat down lotus-style. "The first thing I'd like to say to all of you is that yoga is more than just a series of conditioning poses," Teena said. "It's that, but it's a mindset, too. I don't want you to come to yoga to relax. I want you to relax, then come to yoga."

Is she joking? thought Rose. All of the stressed-out professional women Rose knew who worked between forty and sixty hours a week were lucky if they could drag themselves to a yoga class so they could spend sixty to ninety minutes decompressing. The rest of the time they worked themselves into a frothy lather of frustration. Come to yoga class relaxed? Hardly. Leave yoga class relaxed? Hopefully.

In spite of Teena's expansive girth, she was much more flexible than the rest of them, plus patient and well trained. The hour sped by, and when class ended with the relaxing and comically named corpse pose—during which Yuki fell asleep—they thanked her and told her they were looking forward to the next session.

৩৯৩

Back at her desk, feeling calm and refreshed, Rose attacked the growing pile of mail in her in-tray that was threatening to topple over onto her chair and suffocate her. The first thing she picked up was the front section of *The Globe and Mail*. On the front page a headline screamed: "University Education to Cost $125,000!" The article said that a study had been done estimating that in twenty years, it would cost roughly $125,000 to send a child to university for four years. Experts were recommending that parents sock away

$200 to $300 per child each month from the time the child was born in order to save enough to cover for its post-secondary education.

Good grief. What if your child wanted to be a doctor or a lawyer, or some other profession that takes more than four years of training? No wonder grown children moved back home to live with their parents after they got their degree and started working—they were saddled with such enormous student debt they had no choice. Who could afford to pay rent, never mind sock away some money here and there for a down payment, when you owed the banks and government a big fat bundle?

Rose calculated that if she birthed a baby in the current fiscal year, it would be ready to attend university in eighteen years. That article was speaking to her. There was no way on Earth that she and Jim could save $200 to $300 a month on their current salaries. He hadn't even started contributing to a retirement savings plan yet, and she had been putting in the bare minimum for only a few years.

Of course, there was always the chance—however slight—that Rose's baby wouldn't be smart enough to get into university. Well, she wasn't a snob. There was nothing wrong with taking a trade at a community college or becoming an aesthetician. In fact, Rose thought, that's where the steady money was: you always needed a plumber, an electrician, and a hairdresser.

If, of course, Baby Ainsworth-Mercer did aspire to become a pediatrician, plastic surgeon, or professor, the likelihood of him or her moving back in with Rose and Jim after finishing ten years of post-secondary education in order to pay off student loans, thus interrupting the start of their golden years together, was a distinct possibility.

As far as the pregnancy calculations went, Rose's cons list was starting to outnumber the pros. Surely that would influence her final baby battle plan?

Eight

THAT YEAR, ROSE AND JIM WERE FLYING TO Halifax to spend Christmas with Daisy, Steve, and the kids. Because of the high cost of airfare during the holidays, they usually stayed in their apartment and had turkey dinner with friends, typically Michelle and Shawn, or on their own.

This year was different. On the morning of December twenty-second, Rose and Jim boarded their plane and, two hours later—after a nutritious mid-morning snack of a chocolate bar and a small bag of potato chips—they were welcomed in the arrivals area by Steve, who had left the rest of the family at home decorating gingerbread cookies.

When Rose and Jim followed Steve into the family's white, two-storey, colonial-style house, a ruckus ensued when three short people and one taller one simultaneously threw themselves upon the new arrivals.

"Auntie Rose! Uncle Jim! You're finally here! We've been waiting ages! I have to pee! We made you cookies! I licked the frosting bowl! I got gum in my hair and Mommy had to cut it out with scissors! Santa will be here in two more sleeps!"

The sentences tripped off the tongues of Rose's nieces and nephew in a whoosh of air, although she wasn't sure who'd shouted what. It didn't matter; the feeling of six hands clasped around her knees and waist with such wild and joyous abandon, before they transferred themselves in one unit like a rolling tumbleweed over to Jim's knees, made her heart swell almost as big as the Grinch's when he discovered the true meaning of Christmas.

It was good to be back.

"Welcome home, Rose," said Daisy, as she planted a kiss on her sister's cheek and hugged her warmly, then turned to deliver the same greeting to Jim. Daisy was only fourteen months older than Rose, but sometimes she seemed fourteen years older. Rose thought it was because she had the big-ticket items that Rose didn't: a house, two cars, and three kids.

"Thanks, it's great to be here," Rose replied. "How are Mom and Dad?"

"They're fine. Mom called last night. They're planning to drive up tomorrow morning if the weather's fine and stay at Frank and Patsy's until Boxing Day, so we'll see a bit of them."

Rose and Daisy's parents, Joanne and John, owned and operated a successful company an hour's drive away in Wolfville called J&J Organic Enterprises Ltd., which made and sold pesticide-free foods with creative, hippie-era-inspired names; Bohemian Raspberry Vinaigrette, Frozen Peas Out and Whole Wheat Flour Power were Rose's favourites.

In the early 1970s, shortly before Daisy and Rose started school, the family lived for a couple of years on a commune in a nearby rural community. There, their parents grew organic vegetables and sold them at the farmers' market in town. When their mother wasn't weeding tomatoes, cucumbers, and squash, she was nurturing a lush flower garden; daisies were her favourite. So when their first daughter was born, naming her was easy. Then when they were expecting their second, they decided it would be cute to continue the floral-themed names. It might have been cute in the late sixties—and even for a while into the seventies, when the girls were little—but as teenagers, it was embarassing to be Daisy and Rose.

That was the humble beginning of what Rose and Daisy liked to call the J&J Empire. Without any formal business training, their parents took the organic food industry by storm, long before it became trendy, creating and marketing their own line of products. By the time Daisy and Rose started elementary school in the mid-seventies, the family had moved to the centre of town and their parents had incorporated their business, selling to local grocery stores and maintaining a presence at the farmers' market, which their father insisted made good promotional sense.

In spite of her parents' success, Rose was always disappointed they threw their hippie ideals out the window so easily and quickly. To look at them now, it was hard to picture the sixty-five-year-old couple in their tailored suits once wearing faded denim bell-bottoms, bright tie-dyed T-shirts, and strings of love beads. Rose had seen photographs, so she knew it was true, but she could barely remember those days. Capitalism had captivated them, she supposed. The only holdovers of their former selves were that they still liked the occasional toke, and John refused to cut his ponytail.

After supper, Steve dug out the Monopoly game and set it up on the kitchen table. Katie was doing the one thing she preferred over anything else—acting out stories with her stuffed animals—and Ryan was good-naturedly pestering her, which he preferred doing over anything else.

Ella, who was in the second grade and becoming a better reader every day, hovered at her mother's elbow and read every word from the cards as each person played their turn. When the game was almost over and Rose's score was the lowest, Rose put her head in her hands dramatically and pretended to weep.

Daisy patted Rose's right shoulder reassuringly and Steve patted the left one. Not wanting to miss out on anything the grownups were doing, Ella placed both of her hands over Rose's. "Do you recognize these little hands?" Ella asked.

Everyone burst into laughter, Ella's the loudest of all; she loved to entertain. What Rose always wondered was, where did she come up with her material? It was hard to believe it was original because it was so funny and off the cuff. The saying "out of the mouth of babes" was truly meant for times like this.

When the game was finished, Jim had won, Daisy had come a close second, Steve had trailed third, and Rose had finished last. While Steve put the game away, everyone else moved into the living room. Rose flopped down on the couch. Katie ran over to her and climbed into her lap. Rose knew it would only be a split second before Katie asked her the one question she dreaded: "Do you want to play with me, Auntie Rose?"

There are many things Rose enjoyed doing with the kids that classified as playing. For example, she liked colouring and sticker books, making desserts in the Easy-Bake Oven, putting together puzzles, hide-and-seek, certain card games (Go Fish and Crazy Eights weren't bad), kicking a soccer ball or throwing a Frisbee in the yard, and reading books out loud. The only thing she couldn't stand was what Katie loved most: playing with stuffed animals.

Here's why. Katie didn't just want Rose to have one stuffed animal; she wanted to give her three or four. Then, like a movie director, she wanted to tell Rose what to do with each of them. That type of "playing" would go like this.

"Here Auntie Rose, you be Blue Dog, Horsie, and Scooby-Doo. I'll be everyone else. Now, your three guys come over to my guys' house for supper. They don't have anything to eat at their house, so they're really hungry. But right over here there's a lake, so they can't step on that spot or they might drown. That means they can only walk on this part of the carpet, right? Now get Blue Dog to ask what they are having for supper. No, cut that part and go back. Get Horsie to ask instead."

Katie actually said, "Cut that part." If she didn't end up becoming the female Steven Spielberg of her generation, Rose would eat Blue Dog and Horsie. It wasn't so much Katie's bossiness that bugged her, it was that she didn't understand why she needed her if she insisted on doing all the directing and dialogue herself. As far as Rose could tell, her role was to be a mute puppeteer.

So when Katie asked Rose if she wanted to play with her, and because Rose was tired from the day's travels, she said, "What exactly do you mean by 'play,' honey?"

"*You* know," Katie said slyly, trying to sidestep the answer.

Katie didn't want to spell it out because she knew Rose wouldn't like the answer. She was crafty, all right. And persistent. Even though she knew Rose didn't like playing with her stuffed animals, she never stopped asking. But Rose wasn't going to make it easy for her.

"No, I don't know. Do you mean colouring?"

"No."

"Jigsaw puzzle?"

"No."

"Easy-Bake Oven?"

"No." Katie was getting impatient, but she wasn't going to crack.

"Sticker book?"

"Noooo."

"I know! You want me to read you a book. I'd love to."

"No, Auntie Rose!"

"Then what? I can't think of anything else."

Katie ran the two words together as though they were one, probably figuring that if Rose didn't hear them clearly, she might be more inclined to play.

"Stuffedanimals."

And there it was, Rose thought grimly.

"Katie, you know that's not my favourite thing to play," Rose said, feeling her Best Aunt Status evaporating. "I'm tired from travelling today. Would you mind if we played something else?"

Katie's face had fallen when Rose started her speech, but by the time she finished it had lit up again.

"Okay," Katie said, and Rose could see her trying to come up with an alternative suggestion that was on par to stuffed animals. "How about Dinky cars?"

Now Rose's face lit up. Dinky cars she could handle. You didn't need to have a creative bone in your body to push a tiny vehicle around the floor, right? Just a bit of energy, and Rose thought she could muster enough.

"Okay! That sounds great."

"Yay! Wait right here and I'll go get them," said Katie, clapping her hands together and running upstairs to her bedroom.

When Katie crawled back into Rose's lap, she was carrying a white Dinky car and a pink Dinky car.

Katie looked at Rose sweetly. "Now, do you want to be the pink Dinky car or the white Dinky car?"

The little scamp had suckered Rose. This was the stuffed animal game—but with Dinky cars.

"Neither," Rose said sourly.

"But you said you'd play Dinky cars with me, so you have to pick one."

Katie was right. Rose had said she'd play Dinky cars with her. How could she get out of it without making herself look bad? She decided it was impossible. She would just have to look bad. Katie was five—it was a teachable moment in disappointment, and she'd get over it.

"No, I don't," Rose said. "It sounds exactly like the stuffed animal game except with Dinky cars."

"No, it's different," Katie said indignantly.

"Well, it's not different enough for me."

Rose could see that Katie was trying to think of what to suggest next and drawing a blank.

"Then what do *you* want to play?" Katie asked.

"Nothing," said Rose. "I just want to relax and enjoy everyone's company."

"But you haven't even *started* playing yet!" Katie's lower lip began to tremble.

"Oh, all right," sighed Rose, holding out her hand in defeat. "Give me the pink one." It was then that Rose wondered how much beer Daisy had in the fridge.

Katie was all smiles as she started directing Rose's car up and down Rose's right arm, then her right leg, then onto her head, then over the sofa pillow, then down to the floor. After five minutes, Daisy called out, "Girls! Bath time!"

By nine o'clock, after goodnight hugs and kisses, all three kids were in bed. Steve and Jim were watching TV in the basement family room, and Rose and Daisy were chatting in the living room.

"I've got a Christmas surprise for you," said Daisy.

"Really?" Rose replied excitedly. "What is it?"

"I'm twelve weeks pregnant," answered Daisy, a smile spreading across her face.

There was a moment of silence as Rose digested Daisy's words. Eventually, she managed to make her tongue work again.

"You aren't," said Rose.

"I am," said Daisy.

"But you can't be! I thought Steve got the snip?"

Daisy smiled. "He had been meaning to since after Ryan was born, but you know men—the last thing they want to do is voluntarily make an appointment to see a doctor, never mind for this procedure. He didn't get around to it. But I'm pretty sure he'll go now."

"Is he happy? Are *you* happy? Oh my God, Daisy, you'll have four children. *Four!*"

"Four is only one more than three," Daisy replied matter-of-factly. "When you have this many, one more won't take up much more space or energy. And yes, even though it was a surprise, we're both happy about it."

Rose didn't know what to say. All of a sudden, her vision blurred as her eyes filled with tears. Each time Daisy had announced that she was pregnant Rose had cried, but this time the tears were different. In fact, Rose put her face in her hands and started sobbing quietly.

"Rose, what's wrong? What's the matter?" Daisy asked as she leapt up to get a box of tissues.

"Oh, Daisy, I've been having such a hard time lately," Rose replied through her sobs. "I'm thrilled for you and Steve, I truly am. But I keep having these awful mood swings every time the subject of babies comes up."

"Are you and Jim thinking about having a baby?" Daisy asked gently, placing a comforting hand on Rose's arm.

"We've talked about it a couple of times, but he isn't interested right now," Rose sniffled. "I'm not sure he ever will be."

"What about you?" Daisy asked, studying her sister's face intently.

That made Rose cry even harder.

"I don't know. One minute I think I want to, then the next minute I don't. I feel like I'm the only woman who isn't sure about becoming a mother, which makes me feel like there's something wrong with me. I feel so alone."

"There is absolutely nothing wrong with you, Rose Ainsworth," Daisy said firmly. "For starters, look at your situation. You were over thirty when you got married, you married a younger man who just switched careers, and you live in an expensive city. All of those factors combined would make having a baby right now pretty challenging."

"You don't have to remind me," Rose said, blowing her nose. "I've gone over things in my mind a thousand times. I've even come up with a complicated mathematical formula for when the ideal time to conceive would be."

"When is that?" asked Daisy curiously.

"Right now," Rose replied, bursting into tears again.

"Look, if it makes you feel any better, motherhood isn't always a bed of roses," said Daisy. "In fact, it rarely is. Take me, for example. I loved being a nurse, but Steve and I didn't want a stranger raising our kids. So I'm home full-time, and I can honestly tell you that at some point each day, I go a little crazy. I miss nursing and my friends at the hospital."

"But you wouldn't trade being home with the kids for anything, would you?" Rose asked.

"No, but it's a trade-*off*. And I have to admit that sometimes I'm envious of you."

"Of me? Whatever for? You have a house, two cars, a great husband, three kids—going on four—you have everything. I have nothing."

"That's not true. You're just not looking at what you *do* have in the right light. You live in a city with lots of fun things to do, and you have an interesting job and a wonderful husband. All of that sounds great to me. And, you have the one thing I don't have that I often crave."

"I do?" asked Rose, perking up a bit. "What's that?"

"Freedom. You aren't accountable to anyone but Jim, and he's a grownup who can look after himself. I can't make a single decision for myself without considering how it will affect my children."

It had never occurred to Rose that Daisy might envy her freedom. She had always assumed that her sister loved being a full-time mom because she had never heard her complain about it.

"Sometimes I wish I could just hop on a plane and come visit you for a few days," Daisy continued. "But we're living on one income and we'd have to hire a sitter while I was away, so there's that to consider. And because I took over the household responsibilities when I chose to stay home, I worry that if I'm not here, Steve won't notice when the toilet paper and milk run out. What if one of the kids got sick or hurt and I wasn't home? Could I handle that guilt? I always tell myself that when they get a little older, I'll do it. But I'll be thirty-nine when I have this baby, and that day keeps getting pushed farther away."

"Hey, when is the baby due?" asked Rose. "Do you know if it's a boy or a girl? How are you feeling?"

"I'm due the middle of June, we don't know the sex, and I feel fine," said Daisy, smiling.

Rose snapped out of her funk, shrugging off the negative vibes that were still lingering.

"Daisy, I'm thrilled for you and Steve, and Jim will be too," said Rose. "I want you to know how much we both enjoy spending time with your kids. You and Steve are doing a great job with them."

"Thanks, Rose, that's nice to hear," said Daisy. "And you know the kids love you and Jim to pieces, even when they're being sulky or trying your patience. Ella is especially sassy these days and picking up all sorts of bad habits from the kids in her class. But that's just part of the deal."

Daisy paused before continuing. "You know, Rose, parenthood isn't for everyone, and there's nothing wrong with that. There is no doubt in my mind that you and Jim would make wonderful parents; you've both got good natural instincts with the kids. But just because you *would* be good parents doesn't mean you *should* be. Try to keep that in mind when your indecision is stressing you out."

Rose had never thought of it like that before.

"Besides," Daisy went on, "Steve and I relish your visits. Having you here takes the pressure off us a little. You're great entertainment for the kids, and we know we can go out and leave them with you, and they'll be in good hands. It gives us a break. If you had kids of your own, we'd lose that. And that would be okay, of course. But it would be something we'd miss."

Rose leaned over and put her arms around Daisy. "You're the best big sister in the world. Can I tell Jim?"

"Sure," Daisy said, smiling. "Off you go."

When Rose shared the news with Jim, he slapped Steve soundly on the back and said, "Nice work!" Then he went to the kitchen to get the two of them a beer so they could celebrate man-style.

⁊

Later that night, Rose snuggled against Jim's back in the basement guest room. She asked him what he thought about Daisy and Steve having another baby.

"They've got a shitload of kids already, so what's one more?" Jim replied.

"Can I ask you something?" Rose said, her tone serious.

"You just did," replied Jim, yawning.

"I don't think I've ever asked you this before," said Rose, pausing to work up her courage. "Why *exactly* do you not want children right now?"

Jim was silent. Rose waited.

"Is it because you don't think you're capable of being a good father?" Rose prompted gently.

"No, it isn't that," Jim replied. "I think I'd be a good dad."

"Is it because you don't want to be woken up during the night with a baby?"

"No, that wouldn't bother me either."

"Then what is it?" Rose probed.

"I think it's the weight of the responsibility," said Jim. "I mean, it's a full-time job."

"Does that scare you?"

"Not really. I just don't think I want it."

That's as honest as Jim had been, and Rose couldn't ask for more. But, of course, she did.

"If I got pregnant by accident, would you leave me?"

"Jesus, what kind of a horrible question is that?" Jim said.

"Would you?" Rose pressed.

"No, of course not. But I wouldn't be happy about the situation."

"What if I stopped taking my pills without telling you and I got pregnant?" said Rose.

"That would be a terrible thing to do, and I'm going to pretend you didn't say it," said Jim, his voice a low growl.

Rose sighed. "Don't worry, I wouldn't do that to you. I just wondered what you'd say. Now I know."

"Are we finished this discussion?"

"Yes. But I might want to talk about it again."

"Just as long as it isn't in the middle of the night or before breakfast," replied Jim. And with that, he turned around to face Rose, kissed her on the lips, put his head on the pillow, and went to sleep.

Nine

ON CHRISTMAS EVE, ROSE AND JIM WOKE TO THE sounds of activity in the kitchen above them. Jim got up first and took a shower while Rose made her way to the kitchen to make toast and tea, then realized she had left her birth control pills in her cosmetic case in the upstairs bathroom.

Jim was already in there, so Rose knocked on the door and said, "It's me. Can I come in?"

"Can't a man pee in peace?" he replied, sighing. "Come on in."

"Watch your language, please, there are children in the house," Rose whispered. "I just want to get my pills."

With her right thumbnail, Rose popped a tiny green pill out of its case, tucked it into her palm, and went back downstairs to get a glass of orange juice to wash it down with. On her way past the den, she saw Ella sitting in front of the small TV. She poked her head in the doorway.

"Whatcha watching?" Rose asked.

"Golf," Ella replied.

"Golf? I didn't know you liked golf."

"Yep. I do."

"Since when?"

Ella shrugged her shoulders. "I dunno."

"What is it about golf that you like?"

It was clear that Ella hadn't expected that question. Rose could see her mind working to determine why, exactly, she did like golf.

"Well, it's really interesting," Ella said finally. "For example, did you know that no two putts are ever the same?"

"No, I didn't know that," Rose said, walking over to give Ella a hug and suppressing a laugh. Her eldest niece was going through a phase where when everyone laughed at something she had said, she thought they were making fun of her. She was a sensitive child, much like her aunt. "I'll let you get back to it. I'm going to make some toast."

"Okay," Ella replied, her eyes glued to the screen.

༄

Katie was driving everyone crazy. Out of nowhere, she had started using baby talk. Which was cute when it was coming from a baby but irritating from a five-year-old. The more Daisy and Steve tried to get her to stop, the more she continued.

"Me no like carrots," said Katie when Daisy offered her a baby carrot before lunch.

"You do like carrots, and please speak like a little girl, not a baby," said Daisy.

"Me like to talk this way," argued Katie.

"Katie, that's enough," said Steve sternly.

"Do your friends at school talk like that?" Rose asked, curiously.

"Yup," said Katie, nodding her head as she drove the pink Dinky car over Rose's left foot and up her leg.

Well, that explained it. If you're five years old and in grade primary, to be part of the cool crowd, you have to talk the talk. Baby talk, apparently.

Daisy was planning to make French toast for lunch but after surveying the contents of the fridge, she noticed she was out of milk. Rose and Jim offered to drive to Sobeys.

"Can me come too?" asked Katie.

"If you ask properly," Rose said sternly.

"Can I come too, please?" Katie tried again.

"Of course you can. Go get your boots, coat, and mittens."

Steve passed Jim the keys to the minivan, and Jim, Katie, and Rose piled in. After Rose had secured Katie in her child's seat, they hit the road to the store, which was only five minutes away.

There were several vehicles in the parking lot as people stocked up on enough food to feed an army before the grocery stores closed for two days. Since the pavement was icy, Rose and Katie stayed in the van while Jim went to get the milk.

"Auntie Rose, what kind of a car do you have?" asked Katie.

"Uncle Jim and I don't have a car, honey. We live in a big city, and it's easier to take the bus or the subway than to drive a car."

"What's a subway?"

"It's a type of train, but it only travels inside a city, underneath the ground," Rose explained.

"So you couldn't take the subway from where you live to visit us," said Katie.

"That's right. You'd take a regular train for that. Or a plane, which is faster but costs more."

"That's how you and Uncle Jim came here, right?"

"Right."

"If you ever do get a car, you should get a minivan," said Katie.

"Really? Why's that?"

"Well, because there's lots of room to put kids and stuff."

"But Uncle Jim and I don't have kids," said Rose, wondering where this conversation was headed.

Katie looked at Rose quizzically. "Why not?"

Rose had wondered if this day would ever come, when Ella or Katie looked at her and Jim as more than just their grownup playmates and instead as a married couple who might have children of their own someday.

Rose thought carefully about how to respond in a way that a five-year-old could process. When she started to speak, she looked out the front window.

"Well, there are lots of reasons," Rose began. "Uncle Jim got a new job last year, and he's still getting used to it. We don't have a big house like you live in, just a little place with no backyard or front yard, so there isn't much room for kids. And Uncle Jim and I haven't decided if we're going to have children. But until we make up our mind, we love coming down here and spending time with you, Ella, and Ryan."

Rose thought she had handled that well. She turned around to look at Katie in the back seat, wondering if her niece was absorbing her aunt's words and what kinds of questions she might have next, and how Rose would handle them.

Rose needn't have worried. Katie's eyes were closed and she was humming "Memory," from *Cats*, quietly to herself.

❧

When they returned, John and Joanne Ainsworth's black Volvo was parked in the driveway. Rose braced herself for the encounter. It wasn't that she didn't love her parents, but they were self-absorbed—they loved to talk about their business—so spending time with them was draining.

Rose, Jim, and Katie trooped into the house together. After they had taken off their coats and boots in the mudroom, Katie ran ahead into the living room to hug her grandparents.

"Grandma! Grandpa! You're here!" Katie shouted excitedly. "Did you know that Santa is coming tonight?"

"I heard that rumour," said John. "Have you been a good girl this year?"

"Yes," said Katie primly.

"No, she hasn't," piped up Ella. "She stole a dime out of my piggybank and she hasn't given it back yet."

"I did not!" retorted Katie.

"You did, too!" Ella shot back.

"Girls, Santa can hear you," cautioned Steve.

Ella and Katie stopped talking immediately. They weren't about to put any potential presents in jeopardy. It was too bad Santa didn't come all year long.

"Hi, Mom," Rose said, walking over to embrace her mother.

"Let me look at you," Joanne said, as she held her younger daughter at arm's length. "You look thin. Are you eating properly? Jim, is she eating enough?"

"I'm fine. I'm the same weight I've been for years. Hi, Dad," Rose said, extracting herself from her mother and hugging her father.

"Hi, Rosie," said John, kissing her on the cheek. Rose's father was the only person who could get away with calling her Rosie.

"How are you?" Rose asked.

"Oh, fine, just really busy," replied John. "It's a hectic time for the company, what with the volume of orders for gift baskets. But when business is brisk, I don't complain—there are far worse problems when you're an entrepreneur than being too busy."

"He's not fine, his cholesterol is high," said Joanne snippishly.

"How can your cholesterol be high?" Rose asked, sounding surprised. "It can't be your diet. You eat your own organic food."

"He eats ice cream every day, *that's* his problem," said Joanne before John could get a word in. Rose looked at her father and smiled as he rolled his eyes.

"And he hasn't been exercising," Joanne continued, not giving John a chance to speak for himself. "That treadmill we bought has three feet of dust on it."

"I'm okay, Rosie, really. Dr. Purdy says I've got to cut down on the ice cream and get on that dang treadmill a few times a week. It's nothing to worry about. And besides, your mother isn't one to talk. Her blood pressure is up again."

"I thought you were on medication for that?" Rose asked, lifting an eyebrow in disapproval.

"I was for a while, but when the prescription ran out I didn't refill it. You know I hate taking pills."

"Hmmm," Rose said, but didn't lecture. The way she looked at it, her mother was an adult, and Rose wasn't her doctor. If she wanted her blood pressure to blow up like a hot-air balloon, that was her choice. Not even John could force Joanne to do something when she dug her heels in.

Rose and Joanne went into the dining room to set the table. While they were putting utensils and napkins in their place, Joanne said something that knocked the breath out of Rose.

"It's sad news about Sharon, isn't it?"

Rose had no idea what Joanne was talking about. She hadn't even told Daisy about her falling out with Sharon, and she had no intention of telling her mother, at least not at Christmas. But Rose was going to have to admit that she hadn't the foggiest idea what Joanne meant.

"What news is that, exactly?" Rose asked casually.

"Didn't you hear? No, I suppose you wouldn't have, it happened so recently," Joanne mused. "Last week Sharon had a miscarriage and lost her baby. I ran into her mother at the bank. She said that Sharon's upset, understandably, but at least she wasn't far along and she has Lauren to distract her."

Baby? What baby? From what Rose's mother was saying, Sharon must have gotten pregnant again soon after she had given birth to Lauren. Considering that it had taken Sharon and Peter several years to conceive Lauren with fertility drugs, that was miraculous.

Rose was devastated for Sharon. No matter what their differences were or how long they had been estranged, she could only imagine how traumatic a miscarriage must be, and so close to Christmas—not that there's ever a good time to suffer a loss, but holidays are especially emotionally charged.

Joanne hadn't picked up on any signals that Rose might have sent to indicate that she and Sharon weren't speaking, which was a relief. Rose didn't feel like getting into it with her. If there was one good thing about Joanne, it was that she had never pressured Rose to give her a grandchild. Thanks to Daisy, she had enough of them to keep her occupied.

Rose wondered if Daisy had told their parents that she was pregnant again. She left Joanne's side and walked to the kitchen counter where her sister was dipping pieces of J&J's whole wheat bread into a mixture of eggs, milk, and cinnamon and slapping them onto a skillet on the stove.

"Hey, have you told Mom and Dad about—*you know*," said Rose, lowering her voice and dropping her gaze to look meaningfully at Daisy's belly, which showed no outward signs of an internal presence.

Daisy smiled. "Not yet. I thought I'd tell them when we were all together. Besides, I wanted to let you and Jim know first."

"Thanks," Rose said, grinning at her.

Rose grabbed some glasses and walked back into the dining room to put them on the table. She was still stunned by what Joanne had told her about Sharon. Under normal circumstances, Rose would be there to support her friend. But now she didn't know what to do. Sharon hadn't contacted her, so Rose assumed that she didn't want or need her support. It was probably best at this point that she do nothing, but it wasn't a plan she felt good about.

⊷⊷

John and Joanne were staying for supper, then spending the rest of Christmas Eve at their friends Frank and Patsy's house across town. With Rose and Jim in the house, there was nowhere for them to sleep. They didn't mind; Frank and Patsy were old friends who enjoyed their visits. Plus, it was an opportunity for them to pass a joint around and watch reruns of *M*A*S*H*.

"How are Frank and Patsy?" Rose asked her mother that afternoon as they sipped tea in the living room.

"They're fine. Frank has taken up a new retirement project," said Joanne.

"Oh yeah? What is it?"

"He's building wooden mailboxes."

"That sounds interesting," Rose said, not meaning it. Frank and Patsy were the same age as John and Joanne, but they were retired and didn't have children.

"When are you and Dad going to retire?" Rose asked.

"Well, unless you or Daisy plan to take over the business, probably never," Joanne replied testily, placing her teacup more firmly into its saucer than necessary.

"Don't you want to relax in your golden years?"

"For heaven's sake, Rose, you're talking like we have one foot in the grave," Joanne snapped. "We're still got a few good years left in us, you know."

93

"I wasn't saying you were decrepit," said Rose, trying to calm her mother's ruffled feathers. "I was just wondering if you were planning to step away from the business a little over the next few years. It might be good for both of you, health-wise."

"Nonsense," said Joanne. When she put her foot down, there was no budging her. Rose decided to change the subject.

Draining the last drops from hear teacup, Rose said, "Mom, why didn't Frank and Patsy have children?"

Joanne had been flipping through the pages of a gardening magazine. When Rose's question landed, her right hand hovered above the page for a moment before it dropped.

"I mean, didn't they want any? Or couldn't they have any? I've always wondered," Rose pressed.

"They've never discussed it with me, but I always assumed it was because they couldn't have any," said Joanne. "In our day, you didn't decide whether or not to have children after you got married—you just had them."

"Oh. Well, tell them I said hi."

"I will," said Joanne. And without another word, she turned back to the magazine.

⁶⧾⁹

After supper, Daisy told their parents that she was expecting again. After they got over their initial surprise, they delivered a congratulatory round of hugs and kisses, then left for Frank and Patsy's. Steve, who was a semi-lapsed Catholic—he only attended church during major religious holidays—was taking the girls to the early Christmas Eve mass in town. Daisy, Jim, and Ryan were staying home, but Rose had decided that it might be good for her to go.

Before everyone left, Daisy gave Ryan a bath. When he got out, Daisy put his fire-engine pyjamas on him. He was almost toilet trained, and once he was fully dressed he told Daisy he had to pee. Off came the bottoms, and once he had taken care of business, he refused to put them on again. He ran into the living room and started jumping around behind Katie, who was showing off the new steps she was learning in ballet class.

"Now that is quite a sight," Rose said to Daisy, both of them laughing as they watched a half-naked Ryan imitate Katie's dance moves.

"Yeah, he loves to run around with no bottoms on," said Daisy. "It's embarrassing when a neighbour comes over and he's flying around with his bird hanging out. But it's harmless and he'll outgrow it."

"You hope!" said Rose.

Pretty soon, it was time to get ready for church. Ella and Katie were wearing their best dresses, so Rose went to change out of her jeans and into black dress pants and a blouse.

"What are you going to do while we're gone?" Rose asked Jim.

"Me and my little buddy, here, we're planning an uncle-versus-nephew wrestling match," he said, looking down at Ryan, who had a death grip on his Jim's pant leg.

"Fight!" screamed Ryan.

"Well, don't kill each other," Rose warned as she hugged both of them tightly.

Mass was peaceful, and Rose enjoyed the choir. Katie and Ella behaved, possibly because Rose and Steve had sandwiched themselves between them to prevent talking or fighting. In the pew behind them sat a young woman with what couldn't be more than a six-month-old baby in a sleeper that said *My Very First Christmas* on the front and a matching cap.

Across the aisle was another mother with what looked like a wrinkly newborn. Now and then an infant would cry, drowning out the priest.

It seemed that there wasn't anywhere Rose could go to get away from babies. Not even church was sacred.

᠎◌᠎

When they returned from mass, Ryan was in bed and Daisy and Jim were playing Monopoly at the kitchen table; Daisy was beating Jim, so it was tense because Jim hated to lose. Katie and Ella changed into their pyjamas and got a plate of gingerbread cookies and a glass of milk ready for Santa. They checked to make sure that their stockings were still hanging over the fireplace in the living room and—because they were old enough to know that the sooner they went to bed, the sooner Christmas morning would come—they brushed their teeth without being asked, gave goodnight kisses, and skipped off to bed hand in hand.

While the Monopoly game was nearing its climax, Rose wandered into the den and scanned the bookshelves. She saw something sticking out and pulled it free so she could take a closer look.

When Rose saw what it was, she smiled. It was a small scrapbook she had put together as a Christmas present for Daisy and Steve when Ella was two years old and their only child. Daisy, who was still working back then—she went part-time when Katie was born and then quit for good after Ryan—would send Rose emails with funny Ella stories when she had a quiet moment at the nursing station at the hospital. For six months Rose had printed them at work, then bound them together with a cover page to form the scrapbook she held in her hands.

Rose sat down and opened the scrapbook. The first entry gave her a warm glow.

Ella was in her bedroom with me last weekend and Steve was in the bathroom doing what Steve usually does in the bathroom. Ella marched in and started her usual question-and-answer thing, so I said, "Ella, give Daddy some privacy and come out with Mommy." Ella held out her cupped hands to "give" him some privacy and came out with me. She is so funny that way! The other day, she was yapping at me about something so I said, "Well, you're persistent, I'll give you that." Ella said, "No, Mommy, don't give me that."

What a funny creature Ella had been back then—so smart, so aware. It was too bad that at seven, they were catching glimpses of a sassy mouth—just like her Auntie Rose's. Rose flipped through a few pages and found another gem.

When I called you on the phone last night, Steve put Ella on the other extension. She said, "Oh my gosh!" about something or other, probably repeating one of us, and got a great laugh from you. I said, "Oh my goodness, Ella!" And she said, "Oh my goodness!" I said, "Holy cow!" And, sure enough, she said, "Holy cow!" Then you said, "Say sexy mama." And Ella said, "No she's not."

But it was the last page in the book that tugged hard at Rose's heartstrings.

Ella and I were in her room last night, and I accidentally banged my elbow really hard on her bed frame. I said, "Ouch!" and she asked me what had happened. I told her that I had hit my elbow on her

*bed and it really hurt. She turned right around to
the bed and said, "Don't you do that again, bed,
or I'll bang you." And she hit the bed with her fist.
"Ouch!" she said as she turned to look at me. "It
hurt me, too."*

Rose still found that tale astonishing. Even at the tender
age of two, Ella had the same fierce protectiveness of her
mother that Daisy had of her daughter from the moment
she was born. It was that two-way unconditional love and
loyalty that Rose found so adorable.

୧ळ९

At six-thirty on Christmas morning, three squirming children in flannel pyjamas barged into Rose and Jim's bedroom
and pounced on their bed. Rose was already awake, but Jim
was jolted into consciousness when a little foot planted itself
in his groin.

"What in the name of A-S-S is going on?" Jim shouted.

"Santa was here! Santa was here! Santa was here!" cried
the kids in unison.

"What does *ass* mean?" asked Ella.

"When did you learn to spell?" Jim shot back, surprised.

"Uncle Jim, I'm in second grade," Ella pointed out dryly,
standing up with her hands on her hips and looking at him
like he was a moron.

"Right you are," Jim replied. Then to deflect Ella's curi-
osity about asses, he said, "Now, what's this about Santa?"

Ella grabbed Jim's hand and Katie and Ryan took Rose's
hands; the trio hauled them out of bed and up the stairs to
the living room, where Daisy and Steve were waiting. The
Christmas tree lights were twinkling.

"Presents!" said Ryan, his eyes bulging appreciatively.

98

Steve handed out presents to the kids, who tore off the wrapping paper with wild abandon, while the grownups opened theirs more slowly. Rose took her time between each of her gifts because she wanted to drink in the image of her nieces and nephew unwrapping presents on Christmas morning while they still believed in Santa Claus. As corny as it sounded, it was magical.

An hour later, there was gift wrap all over the living room floor, and everyone had eaten blueberry pancakes drizzled with maple syrup for breakfast. Rose had gotten a good haul of loot, but one present in particular was burning a hole in her brain.

Her mother-in-law had sent her a book of baby names.

Rose tucked the book under a wool scarf the Mercers had also sent; for the time being, she thought it was best if Jim wasn't provoked into taking his mother's name in vain this early on Christmas Day. She'd show him later, perhaps when he was drunk.

John and Joanne arrived at around ten-thirty to help Daisy and Rose with the turkey dinner. At one o'clock, everyone sat down to the feast. The rest of the afternoon, too stuffed to move, the family sat around the living room and watched the kids play with their new toys. Through the big bay window, snowflakes fell softly.

ᑯᑛᑐ

On Boxing Day, all seven family members—eight, if you counted the baby in Daisy's belly—had cabin fever. It had snowed overnight, so Jim went out to brush off the minivan and asked if anyone wanted to go for a drive through town. Ella did—on one condition.

"Will any stores be open today?" she wanted to know.

"Probably not," Rose replied. "Why?"

"I have six dollars and fifty cents, and I might want to buy something."

"But you just got a pile of new stuff for Christmas!" Rose exclaimed. "Why do you want to buy something else now?"

"It's my own life," Ella said saucily, giving Rose a furtive sideways glance to see how she would respond.

Well, now. What could Rose say to that? Nothing clever came to mind, so she kept quiet. Sometimes no response was the best response.

Ella decided to risk the trip anyway and brought her Hello Kitty purse with her, just in case. Lo and behold, the pharmacy in town was open. The three of them trooped inside. Ella knew where she was going; she zoomed over to the display of Beanie Babies.

Rose went with her and looked at the price tags.

"These are pretty expensive, Ella. They're all more than six dollars and fifty cents. Did you want to look at something else?"

"No, I want one of those," said Ella, sticking out her lower lip.

"You don't have enough money," Rose said, fully aware that Ella was expecting her aunt to offer to cough up what she couldn't cover. Because Jim and Rose saw the kids so rarely, they always took them presents, so they were to blame for any expectations the kids had when it came to getting things from them.

Jim wandered over.

"Didja find something you like, Ella?" he inquired.

"Yes, a Beanie Baby, but Auntie Rose says I can't afford it. And I really, really want one." Ella looked up at him with her big, brown, beautiful doe eyes.

If that worked on Jim, Rose would have to try it.

Over Ella's head, Rose was shaking her head back and forth to signal "no." But it was too late; Jim was weakening.

"How much more do you need?" he asked, looking at the price tag. "It's fifteen dollars, so that means you need an extra nine dollars, plus more for tax."

"I have lots of money in my piggybank at home," said Ella.

"You do? I'll tell you what. If I loan you the money right now, do you promise to pay me back as soon as we get home?"

Ella thought about it for half a second.

"Okay," she said quickly, holding out her palm.

Then Ella turned back toward the shelves. She raised her head and spotted something on a higher shelf that was ten times better than a Beanie Baby: a big, fluffy, white unicorn.

"Actually, I changed my mind. I want that instead," Ella said, pointing to the unicorn.

Jim reached up to check the price tag.

"Thirty-five dollars!" he said indignantly. "What a rip-off. It's just a horse with wings and an upside down ice-cream cone sticking out of its head."

Rose decided that the negotiations were over.

"Ella, if you aren't going to buy anything with the money you have, we're going to leave." Then she walked around the counter toward the door. The kid was acting like she didn't have several new toys to play with at home. Enough was enough!

Jim and Ella followed Rose to the van. Ella sulked on the drive home, but Rose didn't let it bother her. Yesterday had been a long and exciting day, and it was probably catching up with her.

When they got back to the house, the first thing Daisy asked was, "How bad was she?"

When Rose was certain that Ella was out of earshot, she said, "Oh, she was fine. She wanted to buy something she couldn't afford and expected us to make up the difference. I kind of knew it was going to happen. When she got pouty, we left the store."

"That was exactly the right thing to do. She's just tired and she was yanking your chain."

"I know," Rose said. "Come to think of it, I'm pretty tired, too."

It's funny. When Daisy and Rose were in high school, their Uncle Doug—their mother's older brother, who had died of a heart attack a couple of years ago—used to say to them, "You two were so cute when you were little. It's such a shame that you had to grow up!"

Rose had always thought that was a terrible thing to say right in front of them, and she had never really understood what he meant—until now.

❦

Two days after Christmas, it was time for Rose and Jim to fly back to Toronto. John and Joanne had left on Boxing Day, stopping by to see everyone one more time before they hit the highway.

When the bags were packed and Steve was loading them into the minivan, Rose tried to steady herself. This was the part she couldn't bear—saying goodbye to this warm house and these huggable bodies. Once they got back to the city, she'd enjoy sleeping in her own bed again and catching up with the girls at work. But this transition tore at her heart.

Rose hugged Daisy first.

"Thanks for everything, I had a great time," Rose said. "Look after yourself and the next Baby Turner."

"We're so glad you and Jim came down," said Daisy, holding her sister tight.

Jim hugged Daisy, then squatted down to squeeze the kids. When he was done, Rose knelt down and opened her arms wide.

"Does anyone have a hug for me?" Rose asked, trying not to cry. She didn't know how long it would be before she saw her nieces and nephew again.

They all rushed at Rose, peppering her with sweet kisses and holding her snugly while they wriggled as she tried to tickle them.

"Now listen, I'm going to keep calling you every Sunday, okay?"

"Okay," said Ella, while the other two heads nodded in unison.

"I love you guys. See you next time," Rose said, waving as she walked out the door with a lump in her throat and tears in her eyes.

Ten

IT DIDN'T TAKE LONG FOR ROSE TO GET BACK into the swing of things in the city. Before she knew it, she was back at work, happy to see the *Dash* gang and hear about their holidays. Rose had pulled Alison into her office first thing to tell her that she was going to be an aunt again.

"Wow, that Daisy is quite...fertile," said Alison. "Was it a surprise?"

"Yes, but she and Steve are both happy about it."

"How do you feel about it?" Alison asked.

"I'm okay, thanks for asking," said Rose gratefully. "When Daisy first told me I was really happy for her but a bit sad for—well, you know, for personal reasons—because it was such a shock. I never thought I'd hear the words 'I'm pregnant' come out of her mouth again. So I wasn't prepared. I did have a mood swing that night, but it didn't last long."

"I'm glad to hear it. And welcome back, by the way."

"Thanks," said Rose, smiling. "It's good to be back."

Rose started sorting through the stack of mail that had piled up during her week away and weeding out the junk emails from the keepers. She had only been at it for a few minutes when there was a light knock on her door. When she looked up, she saw Rima standing at the threshold.

"Hi there. What's up?" Rose asked her.

"Can I come in for a minute?" Rima asked.

"Sure. I don't really want to go through all of this stuff right now, anyway."

Rima came in and closed the door behind her. Then she burst into tears. Rose realized that she wasn't the only one who had been emotional during the holidays.

"Rima! What's wrong?" asked Rose, pulling two tissues out of the box on her desk and handing them over.

"Rose, it was awful. Just awful. A disaster. A big mistake. I'm so humiliated."

Rose waited patiently until Rima had composed herself enough to tell her what was wrong. What Rose had completely forgotten about was that while she was in Halifax, Rima had met what's-his-name, her quasi-fiancé—Mad Max. He had flown in from India with his parents to meet her.

"What was the problem? Did he have a big sty on his eye?"

Rima laughed weakly. That was a good sign.

"No, he's good-looking. After our parents introduced us, we went out for dinner alone so we could talk and learn more about each other," she explained.

"So what did you find out? Is he already married? Does he have a criminal record? An expensive drug habit?"

Rima shook her head woefully. "Worse. He doesn't want children."

"Whaaat?"

"I know. It's terrible, isn't it?"

Rose paused to digest what she had heard.

"Do you mean to tell me that before he came all the way over here from India, you hadn't talked to him on the phone or written him a letter or sent him an email or a fax or a smoke signal mentioning that you couldn't *wait* to have a baby? For God's sake, Rima, that's all you talk about around here!"

"Of course we had communicated," Rima said defensively. "But no, the subject never came up."

"Never came up! Rima, are you nuts? Even Jim and I had that discussion before we got engaged." And a fat lot of good it had done her, she thought to herself, considering that Jim didn't remember it.

"Rose, what am I supposed to do?" cried Rima, the old familiar whine creeping into her voice.

"Do? Forget about him, that's what you're supposed to do," said Rose firmly.

"But what if I can't find anyone else who wants to marry me? He seemed quite decent, except for this one thing."

"Well, it's a pretty big thing," Rose snorted.

"But what if we got married and then he changed his mind? That *might* happen," Rima said hopefully.

Yes it could, and I might be pregnant with quadruplets, Rose said to herself.

"You can't agree to marry a man you only met once in person on the off chance that he might change his mind about an extremely important issue like wanting children," lectured Rose. "I'm telling you, Rima, it's a recipe for disaster. Besides, you're only twenty-seven. You have lots of time to find the right person. Don't your parents have anyone else lined up?"

"Not at the moment. They were hoping this guy would work out because he comes from a very good family." Rima sighed. "But they want grandchildren, so at least they aren't upset that I've broken off the engagement."

"Well, that's good news," Rose replied. "Look, it isn't the end of the world—not even close, in fact. Let me see if I can think of any nice single men I can set you up with."

"Will they be Muslim?" asked Rima, perking up.

"Probably not, but does that really matter if the two of you are in love?"

"I used to think it mattered a lot, but now I'm not so sure," said Rima morosely.

"That's the spirit! You just need to broaden your playing field. Now, I want you to go to the washroom, splash cold water on your face, and forget about Max, because I know there's someone better out there who'll want to knock you up."

Rima blushed and smiled wanly at Rose's blunt assessment. "Thanks, Rose. You've been great."

"No problem. I'm telling you, don't worry about it. It'll happen when the time is right."

Of course, Rose had no idea if that was true, but Rima needed a pep talk, so that's what she gave her.

The only good-looking single guy Rose could think of was Harry, her plumber. *Hmmm.* She might just have to drop an earring down the bathroom sink later this week. When her friends were in need, she was Rose to the Rescue.

After Rima left, Rose turned back to her computer. She deleted several junk messages from her email but stopped when she reached a forward from an unknown sender with the word *happiness* typed into the subject box. As a rule she deleted jokes and anonymous messages without reading them, but for some reason she decided to look at this one. Here's what it said:

We'll be happy when...
We convince ourselves that life will be better after we
get married, have a baby, then another. Then we are
frustrated that the kids aren't old enough and we'll
be more content when they are. After that, we're

frustrated that we have teenagers to deal with. We will certainly be happy when they are out of that stage! We tell ourselves that our life will be complete when our spouse gets his or her act together, when we get a nicer car, when we are able to go on a nice vacation, or when we retire.

The truth is, there's no better time to be happy than right now. If not now, when? Your life will always be filled with challenges.

It's best to admit this to yourself and decide to be happy anyway. Happiness is the way. So treasure every moment you have, and treasure it more because you shared it with someone special enough to spend your time with...and remember that time waits for no one.

So, stop waiting...

until you get married.

until you get a car or home.

until your car or home is paid off.

until you get a new car or home.

until you have a baby.

until your kids leave the house.

until you go back to school.

until you finish school.

until you lose 10 pounds.

until you gain 10 pounds.

until you get a divorce.

until summer.

until spring.

until winter.

until fall.

until you retire.

until you die.

Happiness is a journey, not a destination. So work like you don't need money, love like you've never been hurt, and dance like no one's watching.

'Work like you don't need money?' Ha! Who wrote that, a sadistic billionaire? Aside from that phony baloney, Rose had to admit that the message had merit. Over the past few months, she had spent so much time and energy trying to figure out whether or not she wanted a baby that she hadn't enjoyed the present. What if she got hit by a bus tomorrow? Where would all of that worry have gotten her?

Since Rose was so affected by the message, she decided to forward it to Rima. She was pretty certain that her coworker could use a psychological pick-me-up. She hit the "forward" button, typed Rima's name into the "to" box, and when her email address came up, Rose hit "send." Then, because nature was calling—shouting, more like—she hurried down the hall to the women's washroom.

On the way, Rose passed Rima's office. As she threw a sideways glance through her window, she saw Rima staring sadly at her computer while tears trailed down her cheeks.

⁑

The next morning was Friday. The first week back at work after a holiday was always draining, and Rose was glad it was over. During breakfast, she scanned the headlines on the front page of *The Star* without much interest before turning it over. On the second page, two stories sandwiched side-by-side grabbed her attention. The headline of the first was *Sweden Ranked as Best Place to Have a Baby.* The second screamed *Boy Babies More Difficult to Deliver, Study Finds.*

When did stories about babies become front-section news? In the first one, Canada—which had increased its paid maternity leave from six months to twelve—was ranked the fifth best country to live in out of the thirty-three studied for parents wanting to take time off to raise their newborns. In addition, it was the fifteenth most generous nation for maternity-leave payments.

At the top of the ranking was Sweden, which was the only country in the world to offer couples nearly two years of paid leave to raise their child. Two years! That seemed incredible to Rose. Of that country's ninety-six weeks of paid leave, a year of it is at eighty per cent of full salary.

The other story explained that after studying more than eight thousand births, Irish researchers had found that women were more likely to experience complications during labour and delivery when giving birth to boys. Apparently, among other factors, this was because in general boys have larger heads than girls, which may cause labour to be longer and more difficult.

In that story, the editor of a parenting magazine was quoted as saying that giving birth to her daughter was a breeze compared to the twenty-five hours she spent in the delivery room trying to dislodge her son. After pushing for three hours, a vacuum suction was needed to haul the blockhead out.

Sometimes, it occurred to Rose, she got so caught up in worrying about whether or not she wanted to have a baby that she completely forgot about the actual delivery. When she heard stories like that, she thought that she and Jim should just get a dog.

The researchers discovered that this particular phenomenon could be something specific to male infants, such as perhaps they are less able to withstand stress. No kidding! Rose didn't need an Irish scientist to tell her that. Why do you think women worry so much? Worrying is the way women work things out so their lives will be less stressful.

Guys don't worry one-tenth as much as women do—Rose was positive that was why Jim was able to fall asleep as soon as his head hit the pillow, while she tossed and turned as her brain attempted to calculate potential mortgage, car, and retirement-savings payments two years down the road.

When Rose had digested both her granola and the contents of the articles, she decided that if she couldn't be a Swedish woman having a baby girl, she'd rather the researchers keep the results of their studies to themselves.

⁓

When Rose crawled into bed that night, she knew sleep wouldn't come quickly; her mind was racing faster than an Olympic sprinter. She didn't want to take a sleeping pill, so she'd have to wait until her mental activity calmed down. Besides, she had missed what she called her "window of opportunity" for getting a good night's rest, which falls somewhere between quarter after ten and quarter to eleven. Since it was Friday night, she had stayed up late reading while Jim watched TV. It was twenty after eleven, so it would be a while before she drifted off.

It drove Rose nuts that Jim could fall asleep so fast. As soon as he had given her a goodnight hug and kiss, he was in dreamland. Even if she couldn't see that his eyes were closed, she could hear the change in his breathing.

While Rose was counting sheep—which didn't help but was something to focus on—the bed began to shake. Rhythmically. She groaned as Jim's right leg repeatedly thumped the mattress. Thanks to WebMd.com, a health editor/hypochondriac's best friend, Rose had diagnosed him with restless leg syndrome, which meant that when he was in a deep sleep, he would unconsciously kick the bed. Fortunately it didn't last very long, but it was annoying.

Then again Rose's "window" bugged Jim, so she couldn't complain. He thought she was being ridiculous and that if she really wanted to, she could fall asleep like he did. It wasn't until she printed off a page from WebMd about circadian rhythms and internal sleep clocks that he stopped ranting about it.

Rose also read somewhere that if you shared a double bed with your partner, which they did, if the mattress was divided equally down the middle, the size of one half of it was more narrow than a baby's crib mattress. The article also said that it wasn't uncommon for some couples to sleep in separate rooms because one of them snores louder than a jackhammer cracking concrete. When it came to getting a decent night's shut-eye, Rose and Jim may have had their challenges, but she hoped it would never come to that.

Sometimes Rose read before she went to sleep. Most people read in bed because it makes them tired, but not her. If she was reading something interesting, it put her into a heightened state of alertness and she couldn't stop until she was finished.

That might be why Rose's mind was hopping around like bunnies during mating season. Right before she had turned out the light, she had flipped through the dog-eared pages of *Surrendering to Motherhood* and *The Mother Zone*, two books she had read several times. Both authors write about how having children turned their lives upside down spiritually, physically, and emotionally. They discuss how becoming mothers changed their dynamic with their children's fathers.

Each time Rose reread a passage in one of those books, she realized that she was no closer to finding an answer.

❦

Rose had put off the inevitable long enough. Three months ago, she had gone to the dentist for a cleaning and checkup, and Dr. Belliveau had discovered a cavity. Now, after indulging in too many sweets over Christmas vacation, she was having pain whenever she ate something crunchy, hot, or cold. Since Rose hated needles, she had been avoiding making the appointment. But Jim was getting tired of hearing her complain each time she chewed, so she finally called the dental clinic.

There was a cancellation the following morning at eight-thirty. The less time Rose had to worry about it, the better, so she booked it. Rose had been going to Dr. Belliveau for years, and she knew about her needle phobia; she wouldn't be surprised Rose had waited so long to come in. Most of the time she refused to get her gums frozen while the dentist was drilling, preferring instead to meditate through yoga breathing. Only occasionally, when Dr. Belliveau hit an exposed or tender nerve, did she nearly drop to her knees and beg for a shot of Novocaine.

"So where have you been hiding?" Dr. Belliveau scolded her the following morning as she was sitting in the leather recliner. The hygienist, Heather, clipped a green paper bib around Rose's neck and gave her a pair of plastic safety goggles that were bigger than her head. "I bet that cavity is going to be even more beautiful than it was when I first saw it," said her dentist.

"It's nothing personal, I just wasn't crazy about coming in so you could stab me with a syringe," Rose replied.

"Now, Rose, you know I never inflict any unnecessary pain on you," said Dr. Belliveau kindly as she donned her mask.

"Oh, I know," replied Rose. "It's the necessary pain that concerns me."

"In that case, I've got some news for you. I'm not giving you one needle today."

"Really? That's fabulous!" Rose said, feeling her shoulders creep back down from beneath her ears and her fists unclench. "What've you got instead? A shot of whiskey? A bullet to bite on?"

"Not exactly. I'm not giving you one needle, I'm giving you *two*—one up top and one down below."

Dr. Belliveau and Heather began giggling like they were stoned on laughing gas, enjoying some dental humour at Rose's expense. While they were preparing their pointy instruments of pain, Heather asked Rose what was new.

"Not too much. Jim and I spent Christmas with Daisy and her family, which was fun. Daisy's pregnant again. And I can't decide whether or not I want to have a baby. I guess that's it."

Heather and Dr. Belliveau raised their eyebrows. Both of them were nearing forty and had children: Heather was married and had a seven-year-old son, and Dr. Belliveau had an eleven-year-old daughter whom she had been raising alone for the past year and a half, after her husband had died suddenly from pancreatic cancer.

"Are you planning to fill us in, or what?" asked Heather.

"I'd love to, but I don't want to make you late for your next appointment," said Rose. "You know how I can gab."

"Don't worry about that," said Dr. Belliveau. "We book extra time when you're coming. Dish the dirt."

Rose briefed them on what had been going on. Then she said, "You're both mothers. Any stellar advice?"

Dr. Belliveau spoke first.

"Well, it certainly is a big decision, and one you can't make lightly. And you do have to be prepared for anything, because I had no idea that I'd end up raising April on my own. When you're young and healthy, and you have a loving partner and you make the conscious decision together to get pregnant, you feel invincible. But the truth is, you're not. No one is. So you really have to be prepared to do it, even if it means on your own at some point. My advice is that if you and Jim aren't sure, you're better off waiting until at least one of you is, and then have another discussion."

Rose hadn't taken her eyes off her dentist's while she spoke. "Thanks, that's helpful insight. Another thing I don't understand is how mothers don't worry all the time. Do you know what I think about? That stuff on the news about children, especially young girls, being abducted and—well, you know. I think that if something like that ever happened to my nieces or nephew, I couldn't cope. I can only imagine what a parent would go through."

"If you dwelled on those things, you would drive yourself crazy," said Heather.

"So what do you do? Block it out? Ignore that bad things happen?"

"No, you can't do that, not in this day and age," replied Heather. "In fact, my husband and I just had our first talk with our son about that. Last Saturday, Alex went on his first sleepover at a friend's house; he had slept at his cousins' before. Before he left, Malcolm and I had a talk about Alex's 'personal space,' and how no one has the right to cross over into it. And then we worried all night. But he called us before he went to bed to say he was having a great time, and that made us feel better. You can only do so much for your kids, and then it's up to them."

"Personal space, that's a good way to put it," mused Dr. Belliveau. "I've told April that there are good people and bad people in the world, and that you have to be careful trying to figure out one from the other. If you're a diligent parent, you supervise your child's every move until you feel they're ready to become more independent. I agree with Heather.

My philosophy is that you do the best you can for your child, but at some point you have to trust them and give them some independence when you think they're ready for it."

Rose could have listened to the two women talk about motherhood all morning, especially if it meant prolonging the needles, but there was tooth decay to repair.

In the end, Rose didn't get two needles. She got three. When the left side of her tongue near the lower molar with the cavity refused to freeze, Dr. Belliveau jabbed her again. When Rose protested, the dentist looked at Heather and rolled her eyes.

"Heather, where's the special button on this chair? You know, the *special* button for our *special* patients."

At that point, the triple dose of freezing finally kicked in. It took a lot to render Rose's tongue numb—it was probably the strongest muscle in her body—and she knew that Jim was going to enjoy the couple hours of quiet he'd have that evening. That was okay, she'd just talk twice as much tomorrow.

When Rose got home, there was a vase of flowers on the dining room table. Propped up in front of it was a get well card. Jim was in the kitchen making puréed squash soup for Rose to eat when the freezing wore off.

⁂

The next day at work, Rima said something to Rose that made her burst a blood vessel. Rose had gone to Rima's office to hand her some writers' invoices, and she noticed a new dog calendar hanging on the wall. Rose asked if she had gotten it for Christmas.

"No, I bought it half price after the holidays," said Rima.

"It's so cute," said Rose, flipping the pages to look at the photos. "I love dogs."

"Do you and Jim want a dog?" asked Rima.

"We do, but it'll have to wait till we get a house," Rose replied. Aside from the fact that their landlord didn't allow pets, they'd never coop up a dog in an apartment with no yard, no matter how close the park was. They wanted to adopt a decent-sized dog, a lab or a golden retriever mix, so they'd have to wait until they had more space.

"I guess you guys can have a whole bunch of dogs since you're not having kids," said Rima. "*They* can be your children!"

Rose couldn't believe her ears. Who had told Rima that she and Jim weren't having kids? Rose knew that she hadn't, because the last time she had checked, she was still on the fence. Besides, what sane person believed that a dog was a substitute for a child? Okay, lots of people, but Rose wasn't one of them, as much as she loved dogs.

Rose could feel her blood pressure rising as she tried to keep her cool.

"What makes you say that?" Rose asked, gritting her teeth to avoid saying something she would regret. Rima sure knew how to press Rose's buttons. And although Rima was extremely bright, she could also be as dumb as a post.

Rima looked up at Rose, surprised at the terseness in her voice. "Well, I just assumed..."

"What exactly did you assume? That because I'm thirty-seven and I've been married for a few years, that if I haven't had a baby by now then I'm probably not going to? Or maybe that I can't conceive?" Rose bellowed at her colleague.

No, Rose didn't say any of that. Or bellow. She kept a lid on it. But boy, was she angry.

"Well, I find that odd, because I've never told you that Jim and I weren't going to have children" is what Rose ended up saying. "We're not having them right now, but we might in a few years. We haven't decided yet."

"Oh," was all Rima said as she turned back to her computer, flustered.

Rose stomped back to her office. She was so upset that if she had spoken again at that moment, flames would have shot out of her mouth and incinerated everything within a three-block radius. She sat in her chair and kicked the garbage can, knocking it over. It was childish, but her pent-up fury needed an outlet—and she figured better the garbage can than Rima's shin.

It made Rose wild that for some unknown reason, Rima had made up her mind that Rose wasn't mother material. And she was pretty sure that, regardless of her explanation, Rima would make the same kind of comment again.

The only thing Rose could think of was that for Rima, who couldn't wait to have a baby, any woman who was undecided about motherhood was as good as written off. In her mind, there were only two categories of women: those who wanted children and those who didn't. There wasn't any in-between. Except there was.

⁂

When Rose got home from work, Jim told her that Michelle had called. Rose hadn't heard from her in a while, so she was surprised.

"Did she say what she wanted?" Rose asked, dropping her purse on the floor and running upstairs to change into comfy clothes.

"Something about babysitting Simon," Jim replied, as he dished up spaghetti and meatballs.

Rose quickly pulled on her clothes and ran back downstairs.

"Babysitting? She wants us to babysit?"

"Not us. You."

"Me? Good grief, what's wrong with people today?" Rose shouted.

"What do you mean?" asked Jim cautiously, setting their plates of dinner on the table.

"At work Rima said something to me about having kids that really upset me. And now Michelle wants me to babysit. Do I have a baby-shaped bull's-eye on my forehead?"

"Not that I can see," said Jim.

"Before Michelle had Simon, how many times do you think she babysat other people's kids?"

"Is that a trick question?" Jim asked.

Rose ignored his sarcasm. "I'll tell you—none. She never babysat other people's kids because she didn't like other people's kids. In fact, she didn't like kids at all. But now that she has one of her own, she wants her friends to babysit. Why doesn't she ever get a babysitter so she and Shawn can go out with us? Does *that* ever occur to her? Well, *does* it?" Rose demanded, pounding the table for emphasis, her voice rising.

"Don't know, don't care," said Jim, shovelling forkfuls of food into his mouth.

"Of course it doesn't occur to her," said Rose, answering the question herself. "Because she has completely forgotten what her life was like before she had Simon, and now she expects her friends to do something for her that she never would have done herself. Had everyone gone crazy?"

"I think *you* have," said Jim. "Why don't you just hush up and eat?"

Because Rose was starving, she did exactly that.

While Rose was chewing, she decided that she would call Michelle and tell her that she was busy on whatever night it was that her friend wanted her to babysit. It was slowly dawning on Rose that she wasn't doing herself any favours by being honest with her friends when the topic of conversation was their children. Some lessons, she was discovering, were hard-learned.

Eleven

THE NEXT NIGHT, ROSE DROPPED HER LEAST-favourite earring down the bathroom-sink drain. Then she called Harry, their plumber. Two days after Rose phoned him, she stayed at home to work in the morning so she could wait for him to show up. Harry was twenty-eight, six feet tall, lean, muscular in all the right places and had sparkling blue eyes and short spiky blond hair. He owned his plumbing business, and he was always busy. Plus, he was a good listener, an exceptional quality in a man. His only visible flaws were that he over-gelled his hair and wore a thick gold chain, but that's nothing the love of a good woman couldn't cure.

The last time Harry unclogged a drain a few months ago, his girlfriend had just broken up with him and moved out of his house. Rose remembered scolding him that she thought he worked too much and saying that if he wanted to sustain a healthy relationship, he would have to devote more quality time to it.

Harry had agreed reluctantly, so Rose was curious to find out if he was seeing someone new. If not, she'd have to find a way to introduce him to Rima. After all, both of them were good people who wanted to get married and have kids. Harry had two nephews he adored, and he volunteered at their elementary school one afternoon a week in the library. He owned his house, could unclog drains, loved to read, and volunteered with children. Hello, dreamy Renaissance man!

So when Harry showed up with his toolkit, Rose decided to approach the subject in a mysterious, roundabout way. What came out of her mouth was this.

"So, have you got a new girlfriend?"

Harry looked up from his position underneath the bathroom sink, where he was unscrewing the thing that holds the pipe together with a wrench.

"Nope," Harry replied curtly, looking startled at her line of questioning. "No time to date, too busy working."

"I see," Rose said. *That's excellent news*, she thought to herself. Her mind was racing, trying to come up with a way to introduce Rima into the conversation without being too obvious.

"You know what they say about all work and no play," Rose said.

"I know," Harry replied. "I keep meaning to cut back on my hours, but the demand is there. Besides, I figure if I work flat out until I'm forty-five, I can retire early."

"But that's another, what, sixteen or seventeen years? You'll have one foot in the grave by then if you keep this pace up."

"Yeah, you're right," Harry admitted. "It's hard to meet nice single women, though."

"Aren't some of your clients nice single women?"

"Not too many, actually," Harry said. "In fact, most of them are married."

Married? Like Rose? Was it a stretch, or was Harry hinting that he had a crush on *her*? In spite of herself, Rose felt a crimson flush spread from her neck to her forehead.

My goodness, it was getting hot in the tiny bathroom. Rose walked to the window and opened it a crack. Then she tried to compose herself and remember the real reason for asking Harry to come over, although it had escaped her at that moment.

Oh, yes. That whiny woman she worked with. What was her name? Ruma? No—Rima.

"Well, I work with a woman named Rima," said Rose. "She's your age and gorgeous and smart and single. I think the two of you would hit it off."

So much for the subtle approach. It never had been Rose's top strategy.

Harry laughed. "What are you, her matchmaking service? I'm not into blind dates. Went on one once that didn't go well. Thanks anyway."

"That's okay," Rose said.

That idea had lifted off like a lead balloon. Rose was sure that if Rima and Harry met, there would be chemistry. Actually, she wasn't sure of that at all, but they'd never find out if they didn't meet. She'd have to figure out a way to get the two of them together.

Wait! Rose just had what Oprah called an "aha moment." She would have a party and invite them both. Rose had thrown a grand total of two parties in her life, both surprises—one for Jim's birthday, another for Sharon's. Thinking of Sharon made her sad, so she pushed thoughts of their happy memories aside. She didn't know what kind of party she'd have or when, but it was the only plan she could come up with that might work. Rose to the Rescue, on duty!

At precisely the same second that Rose had her aha moment, Harry cried, "Aha! Here's your earring." Then he dropped an ugly yellow-gold earring that Jim's mother had given her one birthday into Rose's open palm. Apart from the fact that it was gaudy, Rose only wore white gold or sterling silver, so she had been half hoping that Harry wouldn't be able to find it, but honestly, he was that good.

In fact, come to think of it, Harry was great. If Jim was as keen about having kids as Harry was, Rose was certain that she wouldn't be conflicted.

In fact, if Jim ever—God forbid, of course—got fatally knocked down by a speeding bus, car, train, or lawnmower, and Rose had done the proper amount of wifely grieving after laying his cremated remains to rest, she wouldn't hesitate to ask Harry out herself.

Whoa—where had that crazy idea come from? Rose swore that it had popped into her head uninvited. She was shocked at entertaining such a thought. She loved her husband and would never be unfaithful. Which was why Jim was good and dead in her fantasy.

Then it was time for Harry to leave, which Rose hoped would stop further naughty notions from clogging her mind—until the next time their toilet backed up, and Harry had to come over again.

⌘

It was still freezing out. The previous week there had been a huge snowstorm, fifty-two centimetres in one drop, so the snowbanks were even higher than before. It was only the third week of February, which meant that spring was still a couple months away.

To beat the winter blahs, Rose and Jim decided to find some entertainment. Cirque du Soleil was in town for a few days, and they managed to get cheap tickets for a Friday matinee. They left work early to pick up the tickets at the box office. When they arrived, a steady stream of schoolchildren was filing into the theatre.

"I hope we won't be sitting in front of a bunch of rowdy kids," said Jim grumpily.

"What are you going to do, beat them up?" Rose said, laughing. "It's Friday afternoon. We should have realized that kids would be coming. There's no point in getting worked up about it until we find our seats and see who's sitting behind us. So relax for now, all right?"

Jim mumbled something incoherent under his breath, which Rose ignored. They got their tickets and then walked up several staircases, since their seats were in the last row of the third balcony. When they arrived at the correct door, they handed their tickets to the usher, who peered at them closely.

"I'm happy to inform you that because there are so many children attending this afternoon's performance, we're upgrading your tickets to seats on the main floor," she said.

"Really? That's wonderful!" Rose said happily. "Thanks so much."

As they began their downhill descent, Rose poked Jim, who was in front of her on the stairs.

"See, what did I tell you? There was nothing to worry about after all," said Rose smugly.

Jim mumbled something else under his breath, which Rose was pretty sure wasn't "Yes, dear, you're right." Come to think of it, Rose wasn't sure that she had ever heard him use that phrase.

Their new seats were prime, on the orchestra level in the back row, which meant no one was sitting behind them. The theatre was small and the rows were staggered so they had a perfect view of the entire stage. The show was incredible. The performers were so agile and muscular that Rose felt overweight and out of shape. Part of her wished she was still doing gymnastics, and she contemplated joining an adult class.

On Monday morning, since it was cold and snowing lightly, Rose decided to take the subway to work. When she arrived, Kelly, Alison, and Yuki were already there; Rima was at a doctor's appointment, so she was coming in late.

An hour later, Rima knocked on Rose's door. She had gone to Cirque du Soleil the night before Rose and Jim had and wanted to know if they had liked it. When Rose told her about getting the ticket upgrades, Rima opened her mouth and stuck her dainty size-six foot into it.

Rose had described the scores of children who had been streaming into the theatre when she and Jim went to collect their tickets. Rose should have known that she was setting Rima up for one of her favourite lines, but she didn't see it coming.

"Gosh, Rose, if that's how you feel about kids then you really shouldn't have any," said Rima.

Then and there, Rose decided that enough was enough.

"That's not how I 'feel' about kids, Rima," said Rose. "I like children, and so does Jim. We just didn't want anyone kicking our seats and talking through the performance, kids *or* adults. If we ever have kids, we'll be happy to take them to a show like that, and if they want to ask us questions, we'll try to teach them to whisper, but they won't be allowed to kick the back of the seats. I'd appreciate it if you'd stop making insensitive comments. You're awfully quick to tell me why you think I shouldn't have children, and it's upsetting me."

Rima looked like Rose had slapped her in the face. Her eyes opened wide and her face went pale.

"I feel like I've been scolded," Rima said tersely.

"Of course you haven't been scolded—I'm not your mother," Rose replied with a brittle laugh. "But think about it. If—I mean, when—Jim and I have a baby, won't you feel embarrassed after spending so much time telling me why I shouldn't have one? Who are you to judge that decision? How would you feel if I told you that I didn't think you should get married or have kids because I think you're too immature?"

Rose couldn't believe the words that were coming out of her mouth.

"I wouldn't like it at all—and besides, I don't think it's true," Rima said defensively.

"That's exactly how I feel when you say those things to me, and that's exactly why it's important for both of us keep our opinions on these topics to ourselves. Agreed?"

"Yes, I think that's a good idea," said Rima. "I'm sorry, Rose, I had no idea that I was upsetting you." She looked like she was going to cry.

Rose softened a little. "I know you didn't. It's not like you were trying to hurt me intentionally. But now you know how I feel. Can we still be friends?"

Rima smiled weakly. "Yes, of course we can."

"Good. Because there's someone I want you to meet."

"Oh, Rose, is there *really*?" Rima perked up. "Who is it?"

"His name is Harry, and he's my plumber."

"A plumber? Gosh, I don't know, Rose..."

"For Pete's sake, Rima, don't be such a snob. He's gorgeous, successful, single, *and* he wants kids. If I wasn't married, I'd be all over him myself. You have to trust me."

"Really?"

"Yes, really. But since I'm not available and you are"—*and therein lies the tragedy*, Rose thought—"I'm working on a way for the two of you to meet that isn't an obvious set-up, since he's not into blind dates."

"Oh, no, you told him about me?" Rima sounded horrified.

"Well, yes, I kind of had to. Look, don't worry, just leave it with me for now. I'll give you details as they unfold."

"Okay," said Rima skeptically as she got up to leave. "And Rose?"

"Yes?"

"I don't suppose he's Muslim, is he?"

"No, he's not. I think he's Anglican."

"Oh, well...I guess that's okay."

"Look, don't read too much into this yet. All I'm doing is trying to find a way for you two to meet. It doesn't mean you'll like each other."

But, as Rima left, Rose sighed at the thought that her coworker was already daydreaming about her wedding day.

Five minutes later there was another knock on the door. Yuki peeked in. "Can I come in?" she asked tentatively.

"Sure, why not? I didn't plan on actually *working* today," Rose replied. "What's up?"

"Lots, actually," said Yuki slowly. "I need to talk to you about something, but I'm not sure how you'll react."

Rose raised an eyebrow. "Are you thinking about leaving *Dash*? Do you want me to be a reference? If that's it, I don't mind. I jumped jobs enough when I was your age to know what it's like to get itchy feet."

"No, I'm not leaving *Dash*, I like it here. This is something else. It's personal."

"Oh, okay," said Rose, looking up from her computer to give Yuki her full attention. "I'm listening. Shoot."

"I'm pregnant, and I'm not planning to have the baby."

Rose sat quietly, trying to absorb what Yuki had said while letting the shock waves wash over her.

"What?"

"I said I'm pregnant, and I'm not planning to have the baby," repeated Yuki.

Rose thought about the three questions she always asked when she found out a woman was pregnant: How far along are you? How are you feeling? When are you due? This was different.

The pregnancy part was starting to sink in, but Rose was still having trouble with the second part of Yuki's statement.

"You're not planning to *keep* the baby? Is that what you mean?"

"No, Rose," said Yuki wearily. "I'm twenty-three, and most months I can barely pay my rent. I go to raves, where—and I know you don't want to hear this—I sometimes do drugs. I am in no way responsible enough to be pregnant or a mother. I don't want to have this baby, so I'm going to have an abortion. The thing is, I haven't told anyone, not even my closest friends, because I'm afraid it'll get back to my parents, and they'd disown me. But I need some support, and I wanted to ask you if you'd come to the clinic with me."

Sweet Jesus. What was Rose supposed to say? She couldn't think of anything she'd rather do less.

"Of course I'll go with you. But Yuki, have you thought this all the way through? Does the father know?"

"No, and he's not going to, either," Yuki said flatly. "We only had sex once, and it was a big mistake."

"Is it that guy you met the other day?" Rose prompted her gently.

"No. It's a friend's father," Yuki said to a stunned Rose. "And just so you don't have to ask because I know you're thinking it, yes, it was consensual."

"Oh, Yuki," Rise said, trying to not sound disappointed or disapproving. "Aren't you on the pill?"

"Yeah, but I was on antibiotics at the time, and I forgot that they screw up the pill till I missed my period. Then it was too late."

"What about condoms?" Rose couldn't understand how in this day and age, a young sexually active woman like Yuki could get pregnant if she didn't want to. Weren't they teaching sex ed in schools?

"Well, yes, one of those would have been helpful," admitted Yuki. "But unfortunately I didn't plan to have sex that night, and I forgot about the antibiotics, so I wasn't as prepared as I should have been."

"How far along are you?" Rose asked, changing the subject and asking the only one of her three standard questions that felt appropriate. She could guess how Yuki must be feeling, and there wasn't going to be a due date.

"Nine weeks."

"Do you have an appointment booked?" Rose asked.

"Yeah, on Saturday." Today was Wednesday.

"And there's nothing I can do or say that would make you reconsider your options?" said Rose. "You know there are lots of couples who are on long waiting lists to adopt."

"I know, I've thought about all of that, believe me," Yuki replied. "In fact, it's *all* I've thought about since I found out. But I'm not going to change my mind. Rose, I can't have this baby."

Then Yuki started to cry.

Rose was upset about Yuki's decision, but what choice did she have? Yuki didn't need a lecture; she knew she had made a life-altering mistake, and now she was going to have to live with the consequences. If Rose was going to help Yuki get through this, she had to put her personal feelings aside. Going with Yuki to the abortion clinic would be the hardest thing Rose had ever done.

"I'll come with you on Saturday," said Rose, going over to give Yuki a hug as she wiped the tears from her coworker's cheeks with the back of her hand.

"Thanks, Rose. I just want to know that someone is outside the room waiting for me. You don't have to do anything, and I won't ever mention it again."

"Where are you going to go after?" Rose asked.

"I don't want to go back to my apartment. My parents will be away for a few days, so I told them I'd stay there and feed their cat. I'll have the place to myself. I'll be fine." Yuki was trying to sound brave. But Rose knew better.

"I'll see that you get home safely and then if you need me over the weekend, you can call me at home, okay?" Even as she said it, Rose knew she wouldn't hear from Yuki. As independent as Yuki was, Rose could tell that it must have been hard enough for her to ask Rose to go with her to the clinic in the first place, never mind relying on her afterward.

"Thanks, Rose. Really."

Yuki squeezed Rose's hand briefly, then stood up and gave herself a little shake. "Right. I've got work to do."

You poor, foolish, young thing, Rose thought to herself as she watched Yuki walk away.

❧

As much as Rose wanted the next two days to crawl by, Saturday arrived. Rose had told Jim what was going on, and while she could see that he wasn't entirely comfortable with the situation, he didn't try to discourage her from going. He knew it wasn't going to be easy, but they both knew that this wasn't about Rose.

Rose met Yuki at the clinic and then sat restlessly in the waiting room while a nurse led Yuki down the hall and through a door. When she returned after what felt like an eternity to Rose, her face was ashen and she looked like she had been crying. They didn't speak as Rose helped her into a taxi and gave the driver the directions to her parents' house.

When they arrived, Rose went inside with Yuki, waited while she changed into her pyjamas, got her a glass of water and two extra-strength Tylenol, and tucked her into her childhood bed. Then Rose wrote down her cellphone number on a slip of paper and put it next to the glass on the night table. She sat on the side of the bed and leaned over to give Yuki a gentle hug. Rose knew that Yuki wouldn't cry until she was alone.

"Are you going to be okay?" Rose asked.

"I'll be fine," Yuki said firmly.

"Do you promise to call if you need me?" Rose asked.

"I promise. But I'll be fine, really." Even as Yuki uttered those words, Rose knew that they'd never speak of this day again.

Since she couldn't face the subway, Rose called a taxi to take her home. Jim was at the gym, so she walked into the living room and sat on the sofa. Only then did Rose allow her own eyes to fill and overflow.

Twelve

THE GOOD NEWS ABOUT FEBRUARY IS THAT IT'S A short month. Pretty soon it was time to flip the calendar to March. One morning while Rose was eating breakfast, she read an interesting article by a regular columnist who was getting married later in the year who wrote that once she and her fiancé were hitched, they didn't plan to live together full-time. They worked in different cities, so they planned to spend about half of each month together. Rose thought that sounded like a surefire recipe for divorce. It certainly wouldn't work for her and Jim. But then again, Rose had to admit, every relationship was different.

What most bothered Rose about the story was when the writer said that maybe when she had a baby she would want to live with her husband full-time. Rose felt like emailing her to say that if that was her plan, she was in for a big fat surprise—and not a pleasant one. It had taken her and Jim years of living together full-time to get used to each other's quirks and habits. In fact, it was an ongoing process. Rose could just imagine the writer moving in with her husband as she brought their first baby home from the hospital, and the emotional chaos that would ensue.

Good luck, Rose thought. *May the force be with you.*

After supper that night, Rose told Jim about the article. He wanted to read it, so Rose found the page and handed it to him. What she didn't expect was his reaction.

Jim exploded. "Why would you get married if you didn't plan to live with the person you're marrying?"

Rose couldn't help laughing. "Why is it bugging you so much? And for the record, I don't agree with her plan either."

"It makes no sense. Why would she bother getting married at all?" Jim looked genuinely puzzled, so Rose tried to make some sense of it for him.

"Maybe the sacrament of marriage is important to her," Rose said, "but neither she nor her fiancé want to give up their current lifestyles or careers."

"That's bullshit. She sounds like a spoiled princess," said Jim, jabbing his finger at the page. "She says she's messy and she doesn't like to pick up her clothes, make the bed, or do the dishes and her fiancé is neat, which drives her crazy. She needs to grow up, that's what I think."

While Jim was growling, Rose marvelled at how you can spend years with a person and not know everything about them. Until now, she didn't have any idea that Jim didn't consider a marriage to be a "proper" one unless the two spouses shared an address full-time. He seemed to believe that to live separately meant the couple was less committed to the union.

It was reassuring to know that on their fiftieth wedding anniversary, Jim wouldn't announce that he'd be moving into his own place and visiting Rose on Tuesdays, Thursdays, and alternate weekends.

Of course after they had been married fifty years, Jim might want to rethink his position on this topic. Come to think of it, so might Rose.

༺✦༻

At work the next morning, Rose was feeling less than motivated and decided to waste some company time surfing the internet. She logged on to Dr. Phil's website and typed "baby" into the search box. Almost immediately, a list of several baby-related topics came up, including:

Should We Have a Baby?
Questions Your Unborn Child Might Ask
Don't Let Having a Baby Ruin Your Marriage

Rose clicked on the first one, which seemed the most relevant. One paragraph in the *What to Discuss Before Getting Pregnant* section jumped out at her. It said that in order to have a baby, it takes a "yes" from two people, but it only takes a "no" from one person to stop it. Both people need to be comfortable with having a child, so you shouldn't force your partner into parenthood. It could lead to resentment, threaten your relationship, and be bad for the child.

That didn't sound good. Rose and Jim didn't even have a "yes" from one partner. All they had was a wishy-washy "maybe" from her and a "no-way-in-hell-right-now" from him. She kept reading. Dr. Phil said that if you're in disagreement, you must ask yourself whether the problem is not that you're *not* getting an answer, but that you're not getting the answer you *want*. Could you not be hearing your partner's differing opinion? Or could you not be hearing that your partner is not committed to you?

As Rose tried to wrap her head around the confusing double negatives, she decided that Phil was getting too Freudian; either that, or he thought one partner was hearing impaired. He had lost Rose. She decided to ignore that part and keep going. The next section said that a woman shouldn't feel guilty if the desire to have a baby wasn't there—that a lot of women think there's something wrong with them if they don't want to become a mother, but there isn't. It's a big commitment, and if the decision to have a child is a close call, you shouldn't do it. Dr. Phil said that no matter how much you estimate what the sacrifices and demands will be, you won't be anywhere close to the reality.

That was all serious stuff. Next, Rose clicked on *Questions Your Unborn Child Might Ask* and decided she'd write responses for each one:

1) Why would I want to be in your family?

   That's an excellent question. Sometimes I don't even want to be in my family! Is having kind, loving people who like children as parents a good enough answer? Probably not. I'll get back to you.

2) Do you want to have me just so that you can give me a job—to save your marriage, make your spouse settle down, or have someone who will love you? Do you think it's fair to give me a job before I'm even born?

   It is certainly not fair to give you a job before you're even born! When you are tall enough you'll make your bed and wash the dishes in return for a small allowance. Then when you are sixteen you'll get a part-time job. If you're not working full-time by your twenty-fifth birthday and you're still living at home, your father and I will kick you out of the house. It will be for your own good, of course. And to preserve our sanity.

3) Does my other parent want me as much as you do? Or am I going to strain the family in a way that will make you regret having me? Will you resent your spouse for having me?

Yes, you will probably strain the family at first. But your father and I resent each other most of the time anyway, so that's not your fault. I am confident that your father will come around—or I will divorce him—and your mother already has hemorrhoids caused by another type of strain, so that's not a big deal, either.

4) What are your qualifications? Are you mentally, emotionally, physically, and spiritually stable enough to have me? *Cripes! Is anyone?*

Rose was having fun but had to get back to work, so she scanned the last category: *Don't Let Having a Baby Ruin Your Marriage.* Only one point resonated with her, which said that having children is a huge privilege and an awesome responsibility.

That was ironic advice from Dr. Phil—someone who didn't want children himself but whose wife did, and who, after his wife had their first son, got himself fixed. Eventually he had the vasectomy reversed when he realized how much his wife wanted another child, and they had a second son.

Dr. Phil admitted that once to Oprah. Rose thought that it was reassuring to learn that even the good doctor with his PhD in clinical psychology occasionally suffered from marital strife.

No sooner had Rose logged off Dr. Phil's website than Kelly knocked on her door and walked in. Because she was the boss, she never waited to see if it was a good time to talk, even if Rose was on the phone. She'd just barge in and sit down. After Kelly had taken a seat, she handed Rose a stack of first edits to go over. As her left arm stretched out across Rose's desk, she couldn't help but notice the blinding glare of her two-carat Tiffany's diamond solitaire engagement ring. Every time Rose saw it, she swore that her own diamond shrank.

Rose often thought that women compared the size of their diamond rings in the same way that men compared the size of their penises. Women could try to convince themselves that it wasn't the size of the diamond that mattered but rather its quality, but deep down they all want an enormous rock.

So, Kelly had a bigger diamond ring than Rose. But was she happier? Maybe, but then again maybe not.

Rose tried to tear her eyes away from Kelly's ring to pay attention to what she was saying, something about a great aunt of hers who had recently been diagnosed with Alzheimer's disease.

"That's sad news," Rose said sympathetically. Last year she had watched a TV documentary about the condition, which was depressing.

"It is, I know. But at least Great Aunt Catherine doesn't have any children," said Kelly.

"What do you mean by that?" Rose asked, her Insensitive Comment Radar flashing a powerful red alert.

"Well, it could be a lot worse," Kelly said. "At least she won't have to worry about passing the disease on to another generation."

Rose was sure that Great Aunt Catherine wasn't thanking her lucky stars that she didn't have children now that she had Alzheimer's. In fact, she was quite sure that Great Aunt Catherine was devastated by the diagnosis and the fact that she wouldn't have children to care for and visit her. But she bit her tongue and said nothing. Kelly was Rose's boss, and Kelly had been on her best behaviour since her insensitive vacation comment last summer.

Instead of giving Kelly a verbal lashing, Rose told her that she'd call her media-relations contact at the Alzheimer Society and get information on the latest medical research.

Kelly thanked her, sighed, got up, and walked out of the office. Rose also sighed as she watched Kelly walk away. Sometimes she wished she worked with men—she'd deliver a simple "Fuck off" and a flip of her middle finger, then get on with her day.

That night, Jim went to the gym after supper. When he came home, Rose was spread out on her yoga mat in front of the TV in cobra pose and watching a rerun of *Bob and Margaret*. It's the episode where the animated British couple attends a friend's baby shower, and the women give Margaret, who is thirty-nine, a hard time because she and Bob don't want children. The women, who all have kids, pity Margaret even when she insists that she doesn't want a baby and that she and Bob have chosen their careers over children. The women are shocked and disappointed, and Margaret rushes Bob out of there as fast as she can.

Poor Margaret, with her baubly earrings and honker of a nose. Rose could relate, even though her indecision about becoming a mother had nothing to do with advancing her career. Heck, she had been working full-time for fourteen years—she was ready for a change of scenery. She just wasn't sure if she was ready for *that* change.

Jim stood in the doorway watching the show. Rose wondered what was going through his mind, but based on their recent discussions she didn't dare ask. When the show ended, he went upstairs to take off his gym clothes and hop in the shower.

Later that night, Jim's parents called to say that they were planning a visit. They insisted on staying the full two weeks in the apartment with Rose and Jim. *In this tiny, cramped apartment*, thought Rose, *for two weeks?* But you know what? She was okay with that. Her in-laws could stay with them, no problem. She'd move out.

On Saturday Rose had been invited to a baby shower for Michelle, whose due date was imminent. Michelle's friend Lynn, one of the massage therapists she worked with at the clinic, was hosting it, although it was being held at Michelle's house so she didn't have to lug the loot home.

There was a note at the bottom of the invitation saying that Michelle has registered for gifts at the Infant Place. Rose must have been out of the loop because she didn't think that women had showers for second children. Nor did she realize that you could register for baby gifts; she thought that was just for weddings.

After work on Thursday, Rose stopped at the Infant Place and chose three items that were left on the registry: a fitted yellow crib sheet, a soft green blanket, and a package of four facecloths. The grand total came to one hundred and twenty dollars. Rose hoped for the sake of her bank account that Michelle was planning to stop at two.

On Saturday afternoon, Rose walked into Michelle's house clutching a colourful gift bag with decorative tissue peeking out of the top. She could see Michelle's older sister, Marie, in the kitchen putting baby carrots and dip on a platter, and her younger sister, Marlene, stirring a big bowl of what looked like punch.

In the living room, there were eleven more women. Rose recognized Patricia, another massage therapist, a couple of Michelle's cousins, and Michelle's mother. She sat on a folding chair and put her gift bag on the coffee table with the rest of the presents. An older woman around Rose's mother's age who was sitting to her left introduced herself as Mrs. Parker, a next-door neighbour of Michelle's parents and Michelle's childhood babysitter. She seemed friendly, and she started nattering away. She told Rose that she had five children and twelve grandchildren.

Then came the question Rose was dreading. "How many children do you have, dear?" Mrs. Parker asked, her thin, penciled-in eyebrows lifting.

Rose noticed out of the corner of her eye that a few of the women she didn't know turned their heads to look at her when Mrs. Parker spoke.

"I don't have any," Rose said lightly, feeling like she was in junior high and she had answered the teacher's question wrong, and now she was going to get detention. Maybe Rose would have to write *I will have a baby before I'm forty so I will not be ostracized by society for the rest of my life* on the chalkboard a thousand times before she was allowed to go home.

Fortunately, Michelle didn't have a chalkboard. Unless someone had bought her one as a shower gift.

"Oh, dear, I'm so sorry," Mrs. Parker replied loudly, patting Rose's knee. "I just saw your wedding ring and assumed..."

Rose didn't respond. Her heart was starting to race and her palms were perspiring.

"How long have you been married?" Mrs. Parker persisted. Rose wanted to staple her lips shut.

"Four years in July," Rose replied.

"And how old are you?" *The rude old bitch*, Rose thought to herself while trying to stay calm. How would Mrs. Parker like it if Rose asked her how old *she* was? And what had happened to her eyebrows?

"I'm thirty-seven. And a half," Rose added defiantly.

The room went silent. Michelle was still in the kitchen with her sisters, so Rose was on her own. What was she supposed to do now?

141

Mrs. Parker and the other women were strangers. It was none of their fucking business why Rose didn't have children. Then why did she feel like crawling under the couch to hide next to Charlie, Michelle's thirteen-year-old cat?

Rose could hear the wheels in Mrs. Parker's brain grinding. She knew what she was thinking: *That poor girl, she mustn't be able to have children.* Because that was the only explanation she could come up with as to why a married women in her late thirties didn't have any.

To stop Mrs. Nosy Parker from asking any more personal questions, Rose excused herself and went upstairs to the washroom, where she attempted to compose herself. When she came back down, she went into the kitchen hoping to find a friendly face. It was empty except for Patricia, who was married and in her mid-forties. Rose knew that Michelle considered her a good friend.

"Sorry about that bunch in there," Patricia said sympathetically, ladling out a glass of punch. "Want one?"

"Only if there's vodka in it," Rose said, laughing weakly.

Patricia laughed too. "Unfortunately, I think it's the non-alcoholic kind. Anyway, don't let Mrs. Parker get to you. She's a real busybody."

"So I noticed," Rose said dryly as she sipped her punch.

"She said the same things to me when I went to Simon's christening party," Patricia confided. Fortunately, Rose and Jim had been out of town that weekend. "I had uterine cancer a few years ago, so my husband and I can't have children. When I told her that, it shut her up."

"I'm sorry to hear that," Rose said, referring to Patricia's cancer—not the fact that she had managed to shut Mrs. Parker up. "Are you cancer-free now?"

"Five years and counting," Patricia said, smiling broadly. "We thought about adopting, of course, but our hearts weren't really in it. Anyway, I wanted to tell you that I know what you're going through in there."

Patricia drained her glass. "Ready to head back?" She nodded toward the living room, where they could hear the sounds of wrapping paper ripping and delighted oohs and ahs.

"Yes, let's go," Rose said. As they walked down the hall, she realized that Patricia had volunteered her personal details to make Rose feel better and hadn't asked Rose to share hers. She was a class act.

Ten days later, Michelle had her baby. This time it was a girl, and Michelle and Shawn named her Rachel. Shawn sent a group email to everyone with the pertinent details: when labour started, when Michelle's water broke, what time they went to the hospital, how long labour lasted, the time of birth, and Rachel's weight and height. A few days later, an announcement card arrived in the mail with a collage of colour photographs of the baby and the family scanned onto it. They also created a website with family photos, including the new ones of Rachel, and Simon and Rachel even have their own email addresses.

Michelle and Shawn now have the classic nuclear family. Rose was envious of the images of the four of them nesting at home and adjusting to their new family member. She'd give anything to know what that felt like, even for a day.

Thirteen

THERE WERE TWO MORE SNOWSTORMS IN MARCH, then all of a sudden it was April and spring had arrived. On the first Saturday of April, Rose and Jim walked their bikes to the cycle shop for their annual tune-up so they could start riding to work. Rose always felt great about getting her legs and lungs pumping after a winter filled with too little physical activity. The following Saturday they picked up their bikes, and on Monday they both pedalled to work. Rose's ride wasn't long, about twenty minutes, but it was enough to get her juices flowing before she sat in front of her computer for the day.

An hour after Rose had left the apartment, her office phone rang. It was Jim.

"Hey, what's up?" Rose said, happy to hear from him so early in the day. "How was your ride?"

"Don't panic, because I'm all right," Jim began calmly.

"Why would I panic? What do you mean you're all right? What happened? Are you at work?" Rose shouted, panicking.

"I'm at St. Mike's emergency—" Jim started to explain before Rose cut him off with more questions.

"The ER? Why? Would you please tell me what happened?" Rose said, trying not to sob.

"I would if you'd let me get a word in edgewise," Jim replied calmly, although Rose could hear him gritting his teeth.

"I'm sorry, go ahead. I'm listening."

"All right. When I was biking to work, some asshole in a black SUV crowded me at a red light," Jim began.

"'Crowded you'? What exactly do you mean by 'crowded you'?" Rose interrupted.

"He hit me," Jim said matter-of-factly. Rose guessed it was his way of downplaying the seriousness of what had happened, but if anything it upset her even more. She wanted to hear the cold hard facts up front so she could deal with them straight away. "He was turning right on the red, and he got too close."

"Oh my God! Are you bleeding? Do you have any internal injuries? Did you break anything? Do you have a concussion? Were you wearing your helmet?" By now Rose was nearly in tears.

"Calm down. Yes, I'm all right, and yes, I had my helmet on. And it's a good thing, too, because I flipped over the handlebars and landed in the middle of the sidewalk on my head."

Rose started crying, which turned to hiccupping as she tried to catch her breath, while Jim attempted to soothe her over the phone.

"But are you hurt?" asked Rose. Why wouldn't Jim tell her? Was he trying to protect her? Rose's imagination raced. Maybe he had lost an eye but was afraid to tell her. Or maybe it wasn't his eye—maybe one of his legs had to be amputated. If that was the case, she had said "for better or for worse" during their marriage vows, and if the "worse" meant pushing her husband in a wheelchair the rest of their lives, then so be it. Unless they could afford a motorized scooter. Or a prosthesis.

Rose gave herself a mental shake. It was important for her to get a grip on herself and let Jim finish his story. At least he was calling her himself, which was a good sign—if he had a concussion or was in a coma, surely a nurse or the doctor would have contacted her instead.

"I'm a little banged up, but it's nothing that won't heal," Jim answered, the relief evident in his voice. "I didn't break any bones, but my face is a bit bloody, and my knees and hands are scratched. Tore my pants, too. I have three stitches in my left cheek, but the doctor says they shouldn't leave much of a scar."

Rose's stomach removed itself from her throat and returned to its regular position. Over the years she had experienced her own share of similar scares, mainly a result of kamikaze drivers who purposely tried to pick off conscientious cyclists; the irreverent group of bike couriers in the downtown core gave good cyclists a bad name. A couple of times Rose's front tire had gotten stuck in a slippery streetcar track, flipping her sideways into the road and oncoming traffic. She had started to say a prayer every time she swung her leg over the seat before pushing off, and she said another one when she arrived at her destination safely.

"Did you get the guy's licence plate number?" Rose asked hopefully.

"No, everything happened so fast."

"What about witnesses?" Surely someone must have seen something.

"Witnesses?" Jim snorted. "There weren't any. There I

was, sprawled across the sidewalk, and people just stepped over me and went on their merry way like I was a gum wrapper someone had tossed on the ground. That's the big city for you."

"You mean no one stopped to ask if you were okay?" Rose said, flabbergasted.

"That's right," replied Jim.

"I'm so sorry, Jim. How did you get to the hospital?"

"I locked my bike at the corner and flagged a cab."

"Do you want me to come down?"

"No, I'm okay. I didn't have to wait long to see a doctor. I got a tetanus shot and some painkillers, and I called Chris at work to tell him what happened. He told me to go home and take it easy for the rest of the day. That's where I'm headed now."

"Okay, but only if you're sure you don't need me," Rose said. "Will you take a cab and text me when you get home? I'll walk up and bring your bike back tonight."

"Thanks. I'll text when I get home. And Rose?"

"Yes?" Rose held her breath. Maybe he was finally going to tell her about his missing eye or leg. She braced herself.

"I love you."

The shock of what had happened was starting to wear off, and Rose's eyes filled with tears.

"I love you, too," she replied with a lump in her throat.

Rose sat at her desk, thinking about what had happened to Jim. What would she do if she lost him? She'd be alone. Oh, sure, she'd still have her family, but it wouldn't be the same. Sometimes Rose tried to imagine what their life would be like when they were old if she and Jim didn't have children. Would they feel like something was missing? How would she feel when she looked at the Ainsworth family tree with its extended branches—especially Daisy's long one—and saw only her and Jim's names, with no branches extending below them?

If Jim's collision had been fatal, would Rose have wished they had a son or a daughter—maybe with his dimples or dry sense of humour—to carry on their lineage?

Rose thought about her family, in particular her relationship with her mother. Although she had had a happy childhood, she felt that since she had become an adult, Joanne had stopped paying attention to her, which made her sad. It's not that she didn't want to be independent—of course she did. But it would be nice if her mother took more of an interest in her. Rose couldn't understand why someone would have children only to ignore them when they grew up. Was she afraid that she'd repeat the same behaviour with a child of her own?

Rose didn't think so. If anything, she'd probably make new mistakes.

The worst thing about hypothetical questions is that they're impossible to answer with any certainty. Instead, Rose decided to focus on reality: Jim had been hit by a car, and not a single pedestrian had stopped to see if he was injured. Was Toronto somewhere they wanted to live long term? Never mind that unless she and Jim won the lottery, they'd probably be stuck in an apartment forever, since houses in the neighbourhoods they'd consider living in were out of their price range. She wasn't even sure they *had* a price range right now. No matter how hard she tried, she couldn't imagine a future for them there with any positive quality of life. The problem was, she hadn't worked out an alternative to staying.

It was bad enough that summer was only a couple of months away. Rose never looked forward to June, when the heat and humidity began and hung around till September. When she first moved to Toronto two decades ago, the summers were hot but not smoggy or oppressive. Over the past three or four years, however, they had become unbearable. She wasn't sure how much longer she could stand it.

Several times over the years, Rose had wondered what it would be like to move home to Nova Scotia. It would be great to see Daisy and the kids more often—especially with another baby coming—and be closer to her parents as they aged. But what would she do for work? What would Jim do? They had jobs here, and surely the career opportunities there would be limited—although to be fair, Rose hadn't done any research. Would she and Jim feel suffocated after living in a big city for so long?

Rose decided to talk to Jim about it to see how he felt. Maybe it was time for a change. Change could be good. Hard, but good.

☙

When Rose got home from work, she took the stairs two at a time and ran into the apartment. Jim was lying on the couch watching TV. Rose rushed over to him but, before she hugged him, she inspected him from head to toe in order to survey the damage. Yes, his face was scratched. He had forgotten to mention his black eye—it was his left one, but at least he had both of them. There was a bandage on his left cheek covering the stitches. Rose picked up both of his hands tenderly and turned them over to inspect his palms. They were scratched, but not badly. He had put on a pair of gym shorts, and she could see purple bruises on his knees.

"Oh, Jim," Rose said, then leaned over to put her arms around him gently, nuzzling her face into the side of his neck.

"I'm all right," said Jim, stroking her hair. "Don't blubber all over me."

Rose untangled herself from his embrace and looked him in his good eye.

149

"Promise me you'll never ride your bike in the city again," Rose said sternly.

"I can't promise you that, but in the future I'll be extra careful when I'm stopped at traffic lights," Jim replied.

After supper, Rose's mother called. Joanne rarely phoned, and when she did it was usually because she wanted something. This time was no different. She didn't ask Rose how she and Jim were doing, so out of stubborn spite, Rose didn't mention Jim's accident.

Joanne got to the point. "Rose, I need a favour. Our copywriter just left and I've got a deadline for a brochure coming up next week for our pasta line. I don't have time to find someone else, and I wondered if you'd write it for me. I'll pay you, of course."

"Why don't you ask Jim? That's more his thing than mine," Rose said, trying to weasel her way out of doing it and at the same time feeling guilty for suggesting Jim, who would want to work for Joanne even less.

"Because I'd rather boss you around than your husband, that's why," Joanne said with a tinkly laugh, although Rose knew she wasn't joking.

"Mom, you know how I feel about working for you and Dad," Rose said. "I don't think it's a good idea."

"Yes, I know, and I respect that," replied Joanne. "But I'm in a pinch or I wouldn't ask, and my blood pressure has been high so I thought you wouldn't mind doing this for me, just this once. I know you don't want to, that's all right—I'll do it myself on the weekend."

God, Joanne was good. In two sentences she had managed to mix a powerful elixir of manipulation and guilt to try to get exactly what she wanted from Rose. It was so potent that it worked.

"Okay, I'll do it, but just this once," said Rose. "It means

I'll have to work on the weekend, too, you know."

"I know, but you're young and healthy," said Joanne. "You have no idea what a relief this is for me. I'll email you the details and you can send me a first draft on Monday morning. Thanks, Rose."

Rose could tell that Joanne was about to hang up, but before she did she managed to squeeze in a question.

"Are you back on your blood-pressure medication?"

Joanne sighed impatiently. She disliked it when Rose asked about her health. Rose was sure she thought that she was a know-it-all because she was a health editor, and Joanne liked to take her down a peg whenever she could. Rose also knew that in Joanne's own mind, she was invincible.

"I haven't gotten around to getting the prescription refilled. But I will. I've been meaning to go see Dr. Pink for a few weeks."

"Why? What's wrong?" Rose knew her mother, and she never went to her doctor unless something was wrong.

"I've been getting the odd sharp pain in my chest every now and then, and I'm more tired than usual. Maybe I'm just getting old. I'm sure it's nothing to worry about," said Joanne, trying to make light of her ailments.

"Mom, Oprah does shows about women and heart disease all the time. Our symptoms are different than men's, and chest pains and fatigue are two of them. You should book an appointment this week, I'm not kidding," Rose lectured her.

"Oh, Oprah—I mean really, dear," scoffed Joanne skeptically. Rose and her mother don't share opinions on many subjects, the value of Oprah Winfrey to society being one of them.

"Then what about Uncle Doug? Heart disease runs in families. If I were you I'd go see Dr. Pink right away and ask him to give you a stress test and an EKG," said Rose.

"I appreciate your advice, but I'll get around to it when I can fit it into my schedule," said Joanne. "That's the call waiting beeping. I'll be in touch again next week after I've read the brochure."

Joanne hung up. The dial tone buzzed in Rose's ear like an irritating mosquito for a few seconds before she, too, hung up. Rose hadn't had a chance to ask how her father was. Sometimes Rose felt sorry for him; he worked just as hard as Joanne, but Rose didn't think he was as driven. She was sure that he'd take life easier if only Joanne would let him. So much for retirement.

Although Joanne's calculating emotional tactics had upset Rose, she decided not to unload on Jim. Over the years, they had worked very hard—occasionally with professional counselling—to learn how to effectively deal with their families. When they first got together and Rose's parents would get on her nerves, she'd rant about them to Jim so she could get the upset off her chest. What she didn't expect, however, was that Jim's way of supporting her was to jump on the bandwagon and join her in bad-mouthing her parents. That put Rose in an awkward position because although Jim was agreeing with her, she instantly morphed from Dr. Jekyll to Ms. Hyde and felt the need to defend her parents. After all, regardless of their shortcomings, they were the people who had given her life.

Rose's behaviour confused her husband. He couldn't understand how one minute she was raving about how her parents were so wrapped up in their own lives that they had forgotten her twenty-ninth birthday and the next minute she was shouting at him for saying that they were rotten for being thoughtless.

Of course they were thoughtless, but Rose was the only one who was allowed to say so. All she wanted Jim to do was to croon lovingly, "There, there, dear" and give her a comforting hug. And yes, Rose had told him that—many, *many* times—because she knew for a fact that as much as wives would like them to, husbands couldn't read their minds. But that's not what Jim wanted to do. He didn't give a rat's ass about crooning and hugging. If Rose was ranting, he wanted to rant, too.

Invariably those scenarios ended badly, with Rose and Jim feeling misunderstood and with Rose tossing his pillows onto the sofa bed in the office. It even got to the point where as soon as Rose would mention that her parents had called, Jim would say, "I'm not allowed to comment!" and then clam up for the rest of the night. After about a year of this unpleasantness, they finally decided to see a marriage counsellor. Almost all of the couples they knew were going, and although Jim wasn't keen on the idea at first, he was as unhappy as Rose about their fights and committed to finding a way to resolve them peacefully.

Counselling helped, and since then Rose and Jim had come a long way, but it was hard to fight your core personality type. Jim was a debater, and Rose was sensitive. He was opinionated, and she was critical. He had testosterone, and she had estrogen. It was amazing, really, that in spite of their differences they had managed to stay together as long as they had without killing each other. More often than not, marriage was hard work.

Jim's parents weren't perfect, either. His mother was passive-aggressive and regularly made comments when he talked to her on the phone that made him feel guilty for leaving Vancouver, which in turn made Rose feel guilty, since Jim had moved to Toronto to be with her after meeting online and dating long distance for a year. Lately Mrs. Mercer had started needling Rose about giving her a grandchild because she knew better than to bring the issue up with Jim, who would tell her to mind her own business. Rose was too polite to do that, and Mrs. Mercer knew it. Jim's dad was sweet but hard of hearing, loud, and forgetful. He loved to talk, which meant no one else got to, whether you were in the same room or on the other end of the phone. If Rose had heard his stories once, she had heard them a thousand times.

No, Jim's parents weren't perfect. And Rose would soon be reminded of that fact in the flesh, when they arrived in a few days.

Instead of telling Jim about her mother's phone call, Rose went to the kitchen, opened the cupboard where she kept the cookbooks, and pulled out her tattered copy of *The Joy of Cooking*. She tucked it under her arm, trudged upstairs, put on her pyjamas, and crawled into bed. It was only eight o'clock, but there was nothing more comforting than going to bed early and flipping through a cookbook.

Come to think of it, that was one thing Rose and her mother had in common. When Rose was little, they used to sit side-by-side on their living room couch and read cookbooks together, along with *Winnie-the-Pooh* and *The Cat in the Hat*. They shared a fascination for and an admiration of good food. Every time Joanne frustrated Rose, she tried to remember the positive things that her mother had passed down to her. Rose just wished there were more of them.

After salivating over roast chicken and double-fudge brownie recipes, Rose reached over to pick up her cellphone. After three rings, a familiar voice filled her right ear.

"Hello?" said Ella.

"Hi, Sweet Pea," Rose said, smiling.

"Hi, Auntie Rose!"

"What are you doing up at this hour? It's almost nine-thirty there," asked Rose.

"Well, I *was* asleep, but then I had to pee, and after that I needed a drink of water," Ella explained. "I'm going back to bed now."

"Sleep well, honey. Is your mother there?"

"Yep. I'll get her. Goodnight, Auntie Rose," said her oldest niece.

"Goodnight, I love you," Rose said.

"I love you, too. And tell Uncle Jim I love him, too!"

"I will."

Daisy's voice floated down the line. Rose asked her how she was feeling and how her pregnancy was progressing, with only two months left to go. Since Christmas, Rose had been calling Daisy once a week to check on her. Although she had taken an interest in all of her sister's pregnancies, this one seemed extra special. Rose thought that Daisy had sensed it, too.

Fourteen

ALTHOUGH ROSE WOULD NEVER ADMIT IT TO HER mother, she had fun writing the pasta brochure. It was refreshing to work on something besides women's health and fitness topics, and since she loved food, it was an enjoyable experience. It didn't take her long, just one hour on Sunday afternoon while Jim was at the gym. Plus, the money was good; fortunately, John and Joanne were successful enough that they didn't do things on the cheap.

The biggest surprise, however, was that Joanne loved Rose's brochure copy. Rose had been expecting her to pick it apart, but she didn't. She made a couple of solid suggestions, but that was it. If only their personal relationship was that easy.

The week before Jim's parents arrived, Rose decided to take some new jeans she had bought to her tailor, Vincente, to get them hemmed. To say that Rose wasn't clever with a needle and thread would be a gross understatement. If a button fell off a blouse, she safety-pinned it. If a pant leg hem came loose, she duct-taped it. When Rose was in ninth grade, she failed the sewing portion of her home economics course. It took her an entire semester to make an apron, while the other girls breezed through theirs and moved on to A-line skirts. Rose sailed through the cooking classes with top marks, however.

It was in a mood of quiet despair, with the countdown to Rose's in-laws' arrival approaching its final few days, that she visited Vincente. She only saw him two or three times a year, and she always left feeling like a million bucks. His real name was Vincent, and he was as camp and cuddly as her old Teddy Ruxpin. When he opened his shop in Little Italy, he thought it would sound more exotic if he added an "e" to the end of his name—thus pronouncing it "Vin-*chen*-tay"—so he called his business "Vincente's Fine Tailoring."

Vincente always told Rose what fabulous skin she had and how young she looked for her age. He confessed to her once, in a moment of weakness, that he was forty-six but tells people he's thirty-nine. In turn, Rose complimented him on his blond highlights and taut triceps, which bulged out of his designer shirtsleeves. They were good for each other, she and Vincente.

When Rose walked in with her jeans, Vincente was covered to the waistband of his tight Armani black trousers in a frilly white sequined wedding dress and was furiously sewing and snipping.

"Is it wedding season already?" Rose asked, approaching the counter.

"Rosie, it's *always* wedding season," Vincente replied, rolling his eyes. "If I see one more white silk number, I'll puke." Apart from Rose's father, Vincente was the only person who could get away with calling her Rosie. He was a big Rosie O'Donnell fan, so when the name rolled off his tongue the first time they met, she didn't feel the need to correct him.

"You know it pays for your Ferrari," Rose said, laughing.

"Amen to that. Now, what can I do for you today?" Vincente said, standing up from his sewing machine and brushing white threads off his shirt and pants.

"I've got jeans that need to be hemmed," Rose said, stepping into the fitting room as she spoke.

"Well, thank heavens for small mercies and blue denim," said Vincente. "It'll be nice to work on something with colour. How's that gorgeous husband of yours?" Jim had come in once to pick something up for Rose, and Vincente liked his men tall.

"He's fine. His parents are coming to stay with us for two weeks," Rose said, hoping to get some sympathy. Right on cue, Vincente was there for her as she came out of the dressing room.

"Oh, you poor girl. How will you cope? Do you want me to bake you a pan of hash brownies?" Vincente looked genuinely concerned.

"No, thanks, that won't be necessary, I'll just drink instead," Rose said, laughing.

"Now I know you rarely drink, and besides, drinking adds calories, sweetie—and once on the lips, forever on the hips." Vincente tsk-tsked, shaking his head. "If you want to keep that girlish figure, you'll have to come over to the dark side!"

"Vincente, you know I'm too square," said Rose.

"Have it your way, but you don't know what you're missing. When do the out-laws arrive?"

"On Sunday afternoon. It shouldn't be too bad. Jim is taking some time off work but I'm not planning to. They don't really come to see me, anyway. I just hope his mother doesn't bug me too much about giving her a grandchild."

"What's this?" Vincente cocked his right eyebrow. He loved hot gossip. "Are you pregnant?"

"No! That's the problem, as far as Mrs. Mercer is concerned. It's a touchy subject with me at the moment," Rose said without elaborating. She was actually getting tired of talking about her situation, and for her that was quite an admission.

"What exactly *is* the problem?" asked Vincente, as he knelt at Rose's feet and stuck pins into the bottom of a turned-up pant leg.

"Jim and I—but mostly Jim—don't know if we want to have children," explained Rose. "His mother gave me a baby-name book for Christmas, and since then she's been pestering me on the phone trying to find out when we plan to have a baby. I mean, really! It's none of her business."

"When *are* you planning to have a baby?" Vincente didn't care if he stepped over the line. Vincente ignored the line.

"That's just it, we don't know if we are. I've been trying to decide over the past few months. I mean, it's such a serious decision. If we have a baby and then find out that we aren't cut out to be parents, it's not like we can give it away."

"Sure you can, sweetie, you can give it to me. I'll bring up your baby," Vincente said charitably. It was no secret that he was eager to adopt, but his partner—Paulo from Puerto Rico, who was in his early fifties—thought they were too old.

"Thanks, that's kind of you," said Rose. "I'll think about it."

"Good girl," said Vincente, patting Rose's pant leg and standing up. "We're done here. You can take these off."

As Rose returned to the fitting room, she realized that Vincente had managed to pump up her mood, as usual—and then he took it one step further.

"Rosie, have you lost weight?" Vincente asked.

"No, but thanks for asking," Rose said.

"Well, if I haven't told you already, you look fabulous."

Rose should really go there more often. When she said goodbye to Vincente, he gave her an air kiss on both cheeks, told her that her skin was glowing, and wished her luck with her in-laws. Vincente didn't know it, but he did so much more than just hem her pants.

୧୨୦

Hosting company tied Rose up in knots. When someone was coming to stay with her and Jim for an extended period of time, which didn't happen often, she performed tasks that she'd never otherwise do. For example, she took every single item off the bookcase in the office, which doubled as the guest room, and dusted the shelves with a wet sponge. She scrubbed the mould from the bathroom windowsill and the bathtub wall tiles with bleach and an old toothbrush, then took the duvet they kept for guests to the dry cleaners.

There was no question that as far as hosts go, Rose was no Martha Stewart. For starters, she didn't know anything about how to fold a fitted bed sheet or insider trading. Two days before Jim's parents were scheduled to arrive, Rose was so delirious with house cleaning that she almost didn't recognize herself, and she knew that Jim wasn't certain that it really was his wife whizzing around the apartment, washing and ironing the curtains and crawling along the wooden baseboards with a rag soaked in cleanser.

Why, you might be wondering—and rightly so—was Rose going to so much trouble when it was *Jim's* parents and not hers who were coming to visit?

There were two logical answers to that question. (1) If Rose didn't do those things herself, they wouldn't get done. It had taken Rose years to train Jim to take out the garbage and recycling each week, and for him to remember what went out on which days, and to sweep and mop the kitchen floor on Sundays. If Rose gave him additional tasks, his brain would short circuit and she'd have to retrain him, a job for which she had neither the time, interest, nor energy. (2) Mrs. Mercer *was* Martha Stewart.

⁊

By Sunday morning, the apartment was sparkling. Rose, on the other hand, was not—she was limp and exhausted. As far as she was concerned, the amount of cleaning she had done over the past two days should do her for the rest of the year. If she never saw another dirty dishrag again, it would be too soon. Rose warned Jim that if he got fingerprints on anything—walls, kitchen cupboards, closet doors, the phone, or herself—she'd ask him for a divorce in front of his parents. Oh, he'd deny the fingerprints were his, but she'd seen him lick his right index finger so he could turn the newspaper pages.

Rose and Jim took a taxi to the airport to meet his parents. Sam and Alice Mercer were both seventy-two, and although they were in good health, Rose had to remind herself that they were seniors. Neither of them liked to fly, so it was hard to say what state they'd be in when they got off the plane after such a long flight.

"Look, Sam, there's our dear boy!" Alice bellowed from across the arrivals area as she elbowed her husband in the ribs. Alice might be old, but she had a powerful set of lungs beneath her enormous bosom. Sam was pushing a cart full of luggage, and he had more bags slung over his shoulders; he looked like an overloaded Sherpa. How long were they planning to stay, two weeks or two months?

When everyone met in the middle of the crowded lounge, there was hugging and hand-shaking. Alice started to cry, as she always did when she first saw Jim. You'd think that it had been years since she had last set her eyes upon her Golden Boy, when in fact he'd gone home for ten days this time last year.

If this is how a woman who became a first-time mother at the age of forty ended up—needy, clingy, and sobbing over her only child—Rose had better forget it. Hopefully, Alice was the exception and not the rule. And Rose did realize that it must be hard for the Mercers to have their only son live so far away.

Rose and Jim bundled everyone and everything into an airport limo and they all headed to the apartment. When they arrived, Jim showed his parents around, which didn't take long; they seemed to like it, and Alice commented on how tidy it was. Then she started bossing Rose around.

"Rose, dear, would you make us a cup of tea?" Rose gritted her teeth at the missing "please" and put the kettle on, filled the teapot with hot water, and got the tea cozy out, because she knew if she didn't make the tea exactly the way Alice made it at home, she'd never hear the end of it.

"Here, take this and pop two in the pot," Alice said as she opened one of their carry-on bags and pulled out a small box wrapped in cellophane.

"Mom, did you bring tea from home?" Jim asked.

"Yes, dear, I did," his mother replied.

"What else did you bring from home?" asked Jim curiously.

"Not too much. Just the jam we like and some chocolates and mints," Alice said, rooting in the bags and taking inventory. "We also brought our own towels and facecloths so you don't have to do extra laundry."

"How's work, son?" boomed Sam. Jim was a mama's boy, and although he and his father loved each other, they had a hard time finding things to talk about.

"It's great, Dad, thanks."

"Do you miss teaching?"

"Not really. I miss some of the kids and the teachers, but it was a lot of work."

"Hard work never killed anyone, now did it?" said Sam.

"That's true. I work hard at my new job, too. I just minded marking lessons at night and on the weekends. And advertising is something I'd always wanted to try."

Thankfully, the Mercers both agreed that Rose had made a lovely pot of tea. Since it was almost suppertime, Rose and Jim had decided that tonight they'd take them to their favourite pub on Parliament Street. The food was great and there was lots of beer on tap, which would make the Mercers happy.

As they settled into a booth, the Mercers scanned the menus. Rose and Jim usually went there once a week, and they knew what they wanted: a burger and fries for him and a warm spinach salad with chicken and peaches for her. Alice ordered the shepherd's pie, and Sam chose the lamb. After they had polished off their meals and their pints, they were too full for dessert. Since the Mercers were tired after their trip, they decided to head back to the apartment so they could go to bed.

When they returned, Rose went into the office to set up the sofa bed. Alice came with her, lugging one of her suitcases.

"Here, dear, let me help you with that," Alice said, unzipping the bag.

"You don't need to, it's easy to set up," Rose said, going to the linen closet to get a fresh set of sheets, but she didn't stop her. While she was tucking in sheet corners and slipping spare pillows into embroidered shams, Alice was studying the bookcase. At least Rose knew she wouldn't find dust or fingerprints.

"Ah ha! There it is," Alice said, pulling a book from the shelf triumphantly, hugging it to her ample bosom and then showing Rose the cover.

Rose's heart sank. It was the book Alice had given Rose for Christmas. She braced herself for what was coming.

"Rose, sit down here next to me on the bed," Alice said, patting the spot beside her. "Let's have a look at this book while the men are in the living room." She winked at Rose conspiratorially.

"Actually, I should go wash the dishes," Rose said, failing to come up with a better excuse for how she could get out of picking names with her mother-in-law for the baby she might never have. There weren't any dishes in the sink because they had eaten out, but Rose hoped that Alice was too jet-lagged to notice.

Rose needn't have worried. Alice ignored her, grabbed her right arm, pulled her down beside her, and opened the book.

"Let's start at the beginning with the girls' names. I've always loved Amy, it's such a lovely and simple name. And then there's Emma, after my grandmother, God rest her soul."

Alice stopped talking, put the book in her lap, closed her eyes, and placed both hands over her heart as she paused to remember Grandma Emma. Rose said nothing. You don't mess with a seventy-two-year-old Presbyterian saying a silent prayer for the dead.

"Rose, if you found it in your heart to call a baby girl Emma, I would die a happy woman," said Alice, her eyes filling with tears.

Where the hell was Jim? Why wasn't he rescuing her? Rose would deal with him later.

Alice dabbed the corners of her eyes with a linen hankie that she'd pulled from a side pocket of her purse. Then she picked up the book and got back to business.

"Now, what about boys? How about Richard, after Richard Burton? He was a good Presbyterian, you know. Jimmy Stewart was, too—Jimmy has a nice ring to it. There was also Jimmy Carter, who was Baptist, but that can be overlooked."

Rose's head was spinning. If she and Jim had a baby, it would be the two of them who chose the name—and they wouldn't tell anyone what it was until the baby was born. After what felt like two hours but was more like ten minutes, Jim popped his head in the doorway. Rose gave him a look that said, "If you don't help me get away from your mother right now I'll never have sex with you again."

"Dad's ready to go to bed if you two are finished in here," Jim said, grimacing when he saw the book in his mother's hand.

"Yes, we're finished," Rose said. "Goodnight, Alice. I hope you sleep well."

After the Mercers were asleep—Sam was, at least; they could hear him snoring—Rose and Jim stretched out on the living room couch.

"What was going on with you and Mom in there?" Jim asked, nodding toward the office.

"What do you think was going on?" Rose replied. "Your mother wanted to help pick out a name for our baby. When are you going to tell your parents that we might not *have* a baby?"

"Never," Jim said firmly.

"Why the hell not? I hate it when she acts that way—it puts me in an awkward and uncomfortable position. It isn't my place to tell your parents something like that. You need to do it."

"It's none of their business," said Jim.

"It might not be any of their business," said Rose heatedly, "but I'd rather have you let them in on this bit of business if it means it'll get your mother off my back. Why won't you tell them? Are you worried they'll be upset if they think you aren't going to give them a grandchild?"

"Yeah, actually, I am," said Jim. "Look, Rose, my parents are getting older, and you don't see them very often. We haven't decided for sure that we aren't having kids, right? They'll be gone in two weeks. Can't you just put up with it? It isn't hurting anyone if we don't say anything."

But it *was* hurting someone, Rose thought to herself— it was hurting her, and Jim didn't get it. That's because no one was harassing him about whether he wanted to have a baby. Not his friends, nor his family, nor his colleagues—it all landed on Rose. Was it because she was the one with the womb? If so, that wasn't fair. A man could make babies until he was into his eighties if his equipment was in working order. Men's biological clocks had extended-life batteries, while women's were the regular kind—and the more you drained the juice out of them over time, the weaker they got until they finally stopped working.

The badgering wouldn't stop when Jim's parents went home, either, it would continue whenever Rose spoke to Alice on the phone. Next Christmas, instead of a baby-name book, she'd probably send Rose a breast pump. Rose didn't know how much more she could take. Telling Rima off was one thing, but Rose didn't have the same kind of leeway with Jim's parents.

⚬⚬⚬

Fortunately, the fourteen days passed by quickly. While Rose was working, Jim showed Sam and Alice around the city. The Mercers were nervous riding the subway, but they loved the art gallery and the harbourfront. Jim took them to a baseball game and a musical. They seemed to be enjoying themselves.

Alice tried to engage Rose in baby conversations a couple more times, and Rose did her best to divert her. She had decided that Jim might be right—maybe there wasn't any harm in not being completely honest with his parents. Rose felt that she was being deceitful by not being direct, but she was learning that as much as she'd like to, because it was her nature to be an open book, she didn't always have to tell people every detail about what was going on in her life.

Finally, Eviction Day arrived. While the Mercers packed their suitcases, Rose admitted to herself that she was glad they had visited. Considering their age, it might be the last time they travelled to Toronto, which would mean the onus would be on Jim to go to Vancouver to see them.

Rose and Jim saw Sam and Alice off at the airport, and like when they met there two weeks earlier, there were hugs, handshakes, and tears.

"God bless you," said Alice as she hugged Jim hard.

"Take care," Jim said, hugging her back. "Call us when you get home so we'll know you arrived safely."

"We will, son," said Sam, giving Jim a bone-crushing handshake and an equally strong embrace. "Look after each other."

"We will, Dad."

As Rose and Jim watched the Mercers pass through the security gate, Jim cleared his throat.

Rose squeezed his arm. For once she said nothing, because she knew that's what her husband needed.

Fifteen

A FEW DAYS LATER, ROSE WOKE UP WITH A stomach ache. Since it wasn't bad enough to warrant working from home, she took the subway to the office. There was a big planning meeting first thing, and Kelly wanted everyone to attend.

As Rose took her seat at the boardroom table, her knees wobbled weakly and the ache in her stomach got stronger; it seemed to be concentrated on her right side. If Rose didn't know better, she'd suspect that her appendix was acting up, but it had been removed when she was seventeen.

Alison sat down next to Rose. "What's the matter? You don't look so hot."

"I don't feel so hot," Rose admitted, clutching her right side tightly.

Then someone turned the lights out. Or so Rose thought after she woke up.

When Rose opened her eyes, there was a teenager in a white lab coat standing at the foot of the bed. Jim was sitting beside her and holding her hand, and Alison was in a chair on the other side of the bed. An IV was in Rose's left hand, and her right side felt like it was on fire.

"Where am I?" Rose said.

"You're in the hospital," the teenager said kindly.

"Who are you?"

"I'm Dr. Jones, an ER physician."

A doctor! He didn't look old enough to shave. But his age was the least of Rose's worries.

"What happened?"

"You fainted in the planning meeting," explained Alison. "I called an ambulance, and then I called Jim."

"Thanks," Rose said, smiling weakly.

"What are your symptoms?" asked Dr. Jones.

"When I woke up this morning I had a stomach ache, and it got worse as the morning went on," said Rose. "I've got a burning pain in my right side, down near my hip bone, and I feel weak. What do you think it is? And can you give me something for the pain?"

"I'll have to ask you a few questions first. Would you like your friend to give you some privacy?" Dr. Jones said, nodding toward Alison.

"No, she can stay," Rose said.

"That's okay, I'll get some coffee and be back in a few minutes," said Alison, reaching over to squeeze Rose's hand.

"Unfortunately, I can't give you anything for the pain yet because we need to monitor your symptoms," said Dr. Jones. "I know you're feeling uncomfortable, but try to hang on for a while longer."

Uncomfortable? Sure, if you called feeling like someone was stabbing your abdomen with a hot poker "uncomfortable," that's how Rose felt. But she hadn't graduated from medical school—and by the look of this kid, Rose wasn't sure that he had, either.

"Do you still have your appendix?" asked Dr. Jones, furrowing his brow.

"No. Gone."

"Right," said Dr. Jones, making a note on the chart. "Is there any chance you might be pregnant?"

Although Rose didn't mean to, she snorted. "That's highly unlikely," she said, sneaking a sideways glance at Jim, who blushed.

"Right," said the doctor, making another note. "I'll have to send you for a series of tests."

"What kind of tests?" Rose asked anxiously.

"Urine and blood samples, ultrasound, enema, pelvic exam. All routine investigation. It shouldn't take too long."

"Did you say enema? Is that really necessary?" Rose asked.

"I'm afraid it is. We want to rule out any blockages."

Great. It looked like Rose was in for a fun ride at Hotel Hospital.

Two hours later, Rose had been pricked, poked, and prodded by a handful of people in white lab coats. Apparently, her condition was mystifying all of them. Finally, Dr. Jones came back with some news—and with a surgeon called Dr. Thompson, who, much to Rose's relief, had a grey beard and wrinkles.

"We're going to schedule you for exploratory surgery tomorrow morning," said Dr. Thompson. "We suspect you have a twisted ovary, but we need to take a peek inside to make sure."

"What in the name of God is *that*?"

"Well, sometimes an ovary twists. We don't know how or why, we just know that it happens. When it does, it can be quite painful and cause all of the symptoms you're experiencing. If that's what it is, I can put it back in place tomorrow morning. It's fascinating, really. Testicles can twist, too— agonizingly painful, I'm told."

Jim flinched and crossed his legs, then excused himself and headed for the washroom. He didn't handle hospitals well. Neither did Rose, come to think of it. Too bad she was trapped in one.

After the doctors left, Rose closed her eyes and tried to meditate the pain away while thinking about what was happening to her. How could her ovary have twisted? What was it doing in there, the lambada? Why couldn't it sit quietly and behave like a nice, obedient spleen?

Jim and Alison returned together, and then visiting hours ended. Jim was taking the next day off work so he could be with Rose during surgery. Well, not *during* surgery, exactly; Rose didn't think he would have coped well with that. He'd stay in the waiting room until it was over. In the meantime, when he got home he would call Rose's parents and Daisy to let them know what was happening.

⁓

Early the next morning, Dr. Thompson strode into Rose's room and greeted her cheerfully.

"Are you ready, Rose?"

"Yes, let's get it over with," Rose said dryly, as Jim helped her into a wheelchair. "Just make sure you give me lots of drugs."

"Yes, of course. Nothing but the best," wisecracked the surgeon.

When Rose regained consciousness, she was in the recovery room. Jim was back at her side, and Dr. Thompson was perched at the edge of her bed.

"How do you feel?" the surgeon asked.

"Groggy," replied Rose. But she was alert enough to notice that the pain in her right side was gone.

"Are you experiencing any discomfort or pain?" asked Dr. Thompson.

"No," said Rose. "I feel great."

"My suspicion was correct—your right ovary was twisted. It's back to normal now, but while I was flipping it around I found two small cysts, which I removed. Tell me, Rose, do you plan to have children?"

Seriously? What fresh hell was this?

"We're not sure," Rose said, glancing at Jim. "We haven't made a decision yet."

"Can I ask you how old you are?" Dr. Thompson continued.

Could Rose tell the man who had possibly just saved her life that her age was none of his goddamn business?

"Thirty-seven," Rose replied.

"At your age, after what you just went through, I would suggest that if you *are* considering having children, you should start trying to conceive sooner rather than later, because there could be complications. The cysts were harmless, but you never know what's going to develop down the road."

At *her* age? Dr. Thompson made it sound like Rose was ninety-four.

"Thanks, that's good to know," said Rose. What was she supposed to say? Thanks, doc, we'll get right on it as soon as the stitches come out? After promising to check on Rose's incision on his next set of rounds, the surgeon left to see his next patient.

That night, after Jim left and Rose was trying to fall asleep, she couldn't stop mulling over what the surgeon had said—that there was a chance that there could be complications with a late pregnancy. Was it a sign from above that meant Rose wasn't supposed to have children? Or did it mean that she should explore how she felt about adopting?

How *did* she feel about adopting?

Positive, actually. The more Rose thought about it, the more the idea of jetting off to Haiti or Ukraine to rescue an infant from an orphanage seemed heroic and romantic. And costly. Given Rose and Jim's financial situation, she doubted they could afford to even adopt a Canadian baby.

It occurred to Rose that it wasn't the ticking of a biological clock that she was hearing, it was the ticking of a bomb—a reproductive time bomb. She just didn't know when hers was set to detonate. Then a nurse arrived with some pleasant painkillers, and Rose drifted off to sleep.

そうじ

Three nights later, Rose was back home with strict orders from her doctors not to go back to the office for a month. In a couple of weeks, she could start working from home, as long as she didn't spend all day sitting down.

That night, as Rose and Jim got into bed, the thoughts she'd had in her head while she was in the hospital burst from her lips.

"Jim, did you hear what the surgeon said about getting pregnant?"

"Yes, what about it?"

"Well, he said that we should try sooner rather than later, because of my age and the cysts he found on my ovary."

"And?"

The ordeal of the past few days caught up to Rose. Tears filled her eyes.

"Don't you know what kind of time pressure that puts on me? You have the luxury of having lots of time to make up your mind. I don't. What if we wait too long and then it's too late?"

"Do you know what kind of pressure having you constantly bring up this topic puts on *me*?" Jim threw back. "You're just out of the hospital, you're tired and emotional, and now isn't the right time to have this conversation."

"I get the impression that as far as you're concerned, it will never be the right time to have this conversation," said Rose. "If I had known that you didn't want children, I would never have married you. We even had a conversation about having kids before we got engaged, but you don't remember it."

Jim rolled his eyes. "Rose, that was years ago. I can't remember what I had for dinner last week. I just wish you'd stop asking me to predict how I'm going to feel in a year or two, because I don't know. I could kill that doctor for saying what he did."

"He was just being honest," Rose said, sniffling. "I have a right to know."

"Fair enough. But has it ever occurred to you that it shouldn't be this hard to figure out? I think it's fairly obvious that we're not ready to become parents. That doesn't mean never. But it means not now. Why can't you just accept that?"

"I don't know," Rose said sadly, "but I think you should sleep on the sofa tonight."

"Why? What did I do?" said Jim, exasperated.

"Because my incision is sore, and I don't want you to bump into me during the night," Rose replied. That was only half true. Not for the first time, Rose felt that, rather than saying, "When you're ready to have a baby, I'll be ready, too," her husband was telling her to wait for *him* to decide when they would have a baby.

All Rose knew for certain was that she wasn't getting any younger, and she hadn't factored this latest development into her baby plan. Maybe Rose *was* asking Jim for the impossible. As she watched him grab his pillows and walk out of the bedroom, she knew they'd make up in the morning; they always did. Until then, she waited for the painkiller to send her to sleep.

Two weeks later, Rose was moving more spryly, and by the four-week mark she felt like her old self. She was ready to get back to the office, and she knew Kelly would be anxious to have her return soon. After being cooped up at home, Rose couldn't wait.

The following Saturday, she and Jim picked up their old habit of going to the Distillery District for brunch. It had been more than a month since their last visit, and although she wasn't moving as fast as normal, it felt great to stretch her legs in the fresh air again. After browsing around, they stopped to have tea at a café. That's when Rose noticed that Jim was acting strangely. In fact, if she didn't know him better, she would have accused him of flirting with the person sitting behind her. He was definitely making eyes at someone.

"Who are you looking at?" Rose said testily, turning around slowly.

The object of his attention was female, all right—but no more than one year old and sitting in a high chair dropping Cheerios on the floor.

"Oops, sorry," Rose said meekly.

"I should say so," said Jim. "I didn't know I had a jealous wife."

"Well, you *were* making eyes at a younger woman—I just didn't know how much younger," Rose said in her own defense. "Hey, you're not feeling paternal all of a sudden, are you?"

Jim shook his head and sighed. "Why do women have to make things so complicated? Just because I was playing peek-a-boo doesn't mean I want to be a dad."

"No, it doesn't," said Rose. "But it does mean that you have a tender spot somewhere inside of you for children."

"A tender spot, yes," Jim said. "Especially for Ella, Katie, and Ryan. When I'm around them it's the closest I've ever come to wanting my own. But I'm not ready." Jim paused, his Adam's apple bobbing as he swallowed. "If we never have children, would you still be happy being with me?"

Rose couldn't believe they were having this conversation in a coffee shop. So much for personal, private moments.

Rose looked into her husband's eyes and wondered how she should answer Jim's question.

"You know how you say that you can't tell me how you'll feel about having kids in a few years—that you might change your mind and want them or that you might realize you don't?" Rose said. "The same is true for me. I don't know how I'll feel in a few years, either. I guess we should stop trying to predict the future."

"That sounds like a good plan," said Jim. "I know you've been worrying about babies and that I haven't been giving you what you want when it comes to that conversation. Until you wake up one day and tell me that you definitely want to have a baby, I don't think there's anything more for either of us to say about it. Do you?"

Rose thought about that carefully.

"I agree. But that doesn't mean I'll stop thinking or talking about this," Rose cautioned. "And you have to promise me that if you decide one way or the other before I do, you'll tell me right away."

"You'll be the first to know, I promise," said Jim, reaching across the table.

"Thanks," Rose said, squeezing his hand.

On the way home, they stopped at a bookstore. As Rose was fishing around for money in her wallet to pay for a magazine, she heard the cashier saying to the woman ahead of her in line, "Oh, how cute. Is it a boy or a girl?"

Rose could tell that the woman was wearing a baby sling, although she couldn't see the baby. When the woman had bought her book, she turned around to leave the store. That's when Rose saw her "baby."

It wasn't a baby at all. It was a terrier. On the top of its tiny head, a clump of fur was gathered in a pink bow (it was a girl, clearly). Rose paid for the magazine, then walked over to join Jim near the door.

"Did you see that?" Rose asked him.

"Yup," he replied. "Dogs like that should have their legs cut off—they never use them."

"That's a terrible thing to say!" Rose said, although she knew Jim didn't mean it because he loved dogs. Part of her felt sorry for the woman; for all she knew was using her dog as a substitute for the child she could never have. To Rose, it seemed ridiculous to carry a terrier in a baby sling; to the woman, it was probably comforting and natural. Who was Rose to judge her? If it made the woman happy and it wasn't hurting anyone—especially the terrier—then why not?

After they got home, Rose picked up the Saturday *Star*. When she reached page four of the life section, a sensational headline was screaming at her.

Why Wouldn't You Want to Be a Mother? it said. The writer started off by saying that Canadian women were having fewer children than they used to, and that the birthrate was at a "troubling" all-time low. She also said that one in five women in Canada would never become a mother. Then she—for the writer was a "she," and a mother to boot— divided women without children into three categories: (1) the accidental spinster, (2) the "I don't think it's for me," and (3) the "boyfriend said he wasn't ready."

The women in the first category spend their twenties and early thirties working hard and don't get married until they are nearly forty. Then they have trouble conceiving and need fertility treatments. The women in the second group find babies scary and worry they won't be able to juggle work and home. The third group want children but their partners don't.

Rose's blood pressure started climbing as she finished the article. First, why were people still using the word "spinster" in this day and age? Even more infuriating was that in this case, a *woman* had used the outdated term. Second, why was everyone so determined to slot women without children into unflattering, pre-packaged categories? Why didn't people slot women who *became* mothers into unflattering, pre-packaged categories? Where were *those* lists?

Rose decided to compile her own: (1) the accidental mother, (2) the "nothing else matters," (3) the "I'm having a baby whether he likes it or not," and (4) the "I feel sorry for women without children."

Accidental mothers get pregnant by mistake, possibly but not necessarily at a young age. They then spend the rest of their lives resenting their child for the sacrifices they were forced to make and may or may not have more children. If they do, they probably resent them, too.

The "nothing else matters" mothers decided on the day they began ovulating that all that mattered in life was that they birth a child. If they can't, they become depressed and at some point adopt twenty cats or a small terrier they carry around in a baby sling.

The third category consists of women who don't give a rat's ass about whether their partners want a baby or not. They flush their birth control pills down the toilet, and when they tell their boyfriends, husbands, or married lovers that they're pregnant, they explain that the pill is only ninety-nine per cent effective, so there is always that one per cent chance.

The fourth group consists of women who say they are sorry for women who don't have children—whether the woman is happy with her decision to opt out of motherhood or not—because they love being a mother so much that they think those "poor, childless" women are missing out on the greatest joy in life. The women in that group are wasting their energy on misplaced pity and would be better off directing it toward someplace where it's actually needed—Ethiopia, for example, where children are starving and dying of malaria.

And if, as the article's writer said, motherhood was "the greatest joy," why are so many families in counselling? And why are there so many ugly divorces that mess up some kids for the rest of their lives?

Rose dropped the paper onto the floor and, because she felt a headache brewing, closed her eyes. She wanted to tell that writer to forget about the categories, and instead to understand that sometimes women don't have children *just because*. There weren't only three categories—there were as many complex reasons for why women don't have children as there are complex women, and that number is infinite.

Rose was happy for the writer that she loved being a parent so much that she wanted to write about why motherhood was fabulous. If she thought that children were the meaning of life, then good for her. But that was *her* life—what she didn't realize was that the meaning of life could be found in other things, too. And why was it that some women forgot that they enjoyed their lives *before* they had children?

Rose couldn't ponder those questions any longer because Jim came to sit with her on the couch. He had that look in his eye that meant he was in the mood. As he moved in for a kiss, he closed his eyes. For some bizarre reason, Rose thought that this would be the perfect moment to point out that she had read an article about how Sting and his wife practice tantric sex. Apparently they gaze into each other's eyes throughout the event, which is supposed to heighten the experience.

When Rose finished, Jim gazed lovingly into his wife's eyes and said, "I don't give a shit about Sting and his wife." Then he got back to business.

Sixteen

ON JUNE FIFTEENTH, DAISY DELIVERED HER third daughter. She and Steve named her Lulu Rose, which filled Rose's heart. The arrival of Lulu sent her aunt into a tizzy. Rose wasn't sure what possessed her, but as soon as Lulu was born, she felt an instant bond with the eight-pound, eight-ounce miracle who shared her name.

When Daisy called from the hospital to tell Rose that Lulu had entered the world safely, Rose burst into tears. She had also cried when Ella, Katie, and Ryan were born, but this felt different, although Rose couldn't pinpoint why. It wasn't maternal instinct that was washing over her—how could she feel maternal about a baby she had yet to meet?

No, it was something else, a sensation that was more difficult to define. It wasn't like Rose felt that Lulu was hers, but she did sense that the two of them were going to have a special relationship. And it wasn't that she would love Ella, Katie, and Ryan any less. It's just that when Lulu arrived, Rose was at such an unsettled place in her life that Lulu's birth gave her a new perspective, whether she had expected it to or not.

As soon as Lulu was born, Rose started to feel strange— happier. In fact, all of a sudden she felt better than she had in months. There was something about the birth of a baby who shared some of her own genetic makeup, in whatever small way, that made life look rosier. Rose started to feel Rosier, too—more like her old self before she had suffered her first attack of baby fever what seemed like a million years ago but had only been ten months.

It's not like Rose no longer thought about Sharon. She did, and she still missed their friendship. Did Rose have any regrets about what had taken place between them? Of course. Rose often wondered if Sharon had recovered from her miscarriage.

With the clarity of hindsight, Rose wished that she had waited until Lauren was a few months old instead of a few weeks old to reveal her feelings to Sharon. And she wished that she hadn't sent her an email, which was a lousy way to handle relationship problems. But although she understood that Sharon had probably been hormonal at the time, Rose had been hormonal, too. If you're a woman, you don't need to have a baby to let the estrogen coursing through your veins get the better of you. Rose couldn't have stopped last year's pre-birthday baby angst from happening any more than Sharon could have changed her reaction to Rose's email. Rose knew that now, but did Sharon?

The sad thing was that neither Sharon nor Rose had tried to patch things up. Rose couldn't because she was too afraid. Sharon had said hurtful things in her message, and Rose didn't want to open herself up to more emotional bruising. This had been their first serious fight, and Rose had no idea how to resolve it, or even if it was worth trying. If Sharon had become as self-absorbed as she had been throughout her pregnancy and as callous as her email had suggested, did Rose want her back in her life?

At the end of June, Jim won a national advertising award for one of his campaigns. A month later, he came home from work all hyped up.

"You'll never guess what happened today," said Jim excitedly, dropping his briefcase on the floor and walking into the kitchen to give Rose a hug and kiss.

"Hmmm, let me think," said Rose. "You won another award?"

"No, but it has to do with the one I already won," Jim replied, beaming.

"You'd better tell me before you burst," Rose said, laughing.

"Right before I left work tonight, Chris called me into his office." Chris was his boss at Creative Communications.

"What did he want?" Rose asked, raising an eyebrow and trying to give him her full attention while dicing a carrot.

"That's just it, you'll never guess in a million years. He wanted to tell me that he was thinking about promoting me before I won the award, and then it was a done deal."

"That's amazing!" Rose shouted, wiping her hands on her apron and walking around the kitchen counter to give him a hug and kiss. "You've worked really hard this past year, and if anyone deserves a promotion, it's you. Congratulations, honey."

"Thanks, but hold on—that's only the first part of the good news. The second part has to do with the promotion."

Rose wished that Jim would spit out the whole story in one go instead of drawing it out to heighten the suspense.

"What about the promotion, then? Are you going to be a senior copywriter?"

"Yes, I am. But you'll never guess where." Jim was grinning from ear to ear.

"I give up. Where?"

"At the company's new office—in Halifax."

Rose jaw dropped. "Are you kidding?" she said, trying to absorb the news.

"I'm not. If I decide to accept the offer, we have to be packed up and moved by the first of October. What do you think?"

What *did* she think?

Rose thought it sounded like a wonderful opportunity for Jim. But for the moment, she held her tongue.

"Do *you* want to move?" Rose asked Jim.

"Sure, why not? I've had enough of big-city life. And just think—I'll be making more money and the cost of living will be lower. We could buy a house *and* a car." Jim's eyes were glazing over, and Rose knew he was sold on the idea. After his bike accident, who was Rose kidding—so was she.

After supper, Rose and Jim lay on the sofa and talked about the pros and cons of moving. The pros list was easy to compile. They would see Daisy, Steve, and the kids regularly, which was a big bonus, especially now that Lulu was part of the family. The summers wouldn't be smoggy, and they'd be close to the ocean. There was a vibrant arts community, so they'd still be able to attend the theatre, symphony, and concerts.

Even though Rose and Jim hadn't discussed the topic recently, she couldn't help but think that raising children in a small city had many advantages over bringing them up in a big one.

The cons list was more troublesome. Although it was an amazing career opportunity for Jim, Rose would have to give up the job she loved and freelance full-time, which scared her. She didn't know anyone in the publishing industry back home, so it would be tough starting out. When the time was right,

Rose decided to ask Kelly if she would be willing to keep her on at *Dash* as a regular contributing editor and writer, which would at least give her some consistent work.

The biggest downside was that Rose would have to leave the friends, colleagues, and health-care providers she had gotten to know over the years. What would she do without Dr. Davies, Dr. Belliveau, and Heather? And Vincente? As for friends like Michelle, the truth was that she didn't see her much anymore. She'd miss the *Dash* girls, but hopefully people would visit them after they got settled—it wasn't like they were moving to the North Pole.

After a couple hours of discussion, Rose and Jim had made up their minds: they would go for it! Jim would accept the promotion, and in three months they would move and the next chapter of their lives would begin. When they went to bed that night, Rose's mind was racing; she was excited at what lay ahead yet scared of the risks.

Eventually, Rose's thoughts settled down and she fell asleep. Her dreams were filled with cardboard boxes sealed with packing tape floating on ocean waves.

❧

The next day, Jim met with Chris to accept his promotion. That night, Rose called Daisy and told her their news—Daisy was surprised and thrilled. Rose asked if Steve could see if any of his colleagues had a lead on a two-bedroom apartment in a house, and Daisy said he'd be in touch when he had something to report.

Rose and Jim had decided to rent an apartment so they could save money and look for a house after they were settled. They planned to wait until the end of July to give their notice to their landlord, which was when Rose would tell Kelly, too. She thought that would give her boss lots of time to figure out how she could keep Rose on staff on a part-time basis. At least Rose would be there to see the magazine through the busy summer production schedule. Everything seemed to be falling into place.

Later that week, Rose got an email at work from Steve, who had come up with a great lead—someone had a friend who was a medical student and who was moving to a new place on the first of October; he and his girlfriend had been renting the upper flat in a Victorian house in Halifax's South End. Steve had forwarded the rental-listing details, which contained some exterior and interior shots. It was a two-bedroom apartment plus a den, and it had a deck off the eat-in kitchen, a dining room, a washer and dryer in the bathroom, and a spacious, sunny living room. The rent was reasonable, and they'd only have to pay for electricity.

Not only was the place beautiful, but it was also afford-able. The apartment was bigger than their current one and cost four hundred dollars less a month. The downstairs neighbours were a married couple, both retired university professors. Rose forwarded the email to Jim at work, who sent this brief reply five minutes later: *Where do we sign?*

There was an email address listed for Robert Rideout, the landlord, so Rose fired off a message and crossed her fingers. Right before she shut down her computer to go home, she checked her email. There it was—a reply! Rose's heart was pounding as she clicked on the message and read its contents:

Dear Ms. Ainsworth,
You and your husband sound like ideal candidates for the flat. I'm looking for quiet, mature, profes-sional people with no pets and who don't smoke. I don't have a problem with you working from home, as many young people seem to these days. Your

*downstairs neighbours are quiet and out most of the
day doing volunteer work and enjoying a variety of
hobbies. I think the place will suit you well.*

*If you could please forward two references I'll
contact them, and if everything checks out I'll email
you the lease to sign. Then I would require the first
month's rent in advance as a security deposit. If this
arrangement suits you, we have a deal.*
Sincerely, Robert Rideout

Mr. Rideout sounded nice. Rose guessed he was an older
gentleman from his use of the phrases "Ms. Ainsworth"
and "young people." After finding the phone numbers of
their previous two landlords, Rose typed a reply with the
requested information, then hit send. If all went well, they
could have the apartment sorted out by the end of the week.
Then they just had to find affordable movers. Jim could look
after that.

Then the packing would begin. Rose had only one thing
to say about that—she hated packing. But if there was one
thing she had learned over the years, it was that the sooner
you began tossing your belongings into boxes, the better.
They'd start in August.

On Friday, Mr. Rideout called Rose at work: the apartment was theirs if they wanted it. Rose was relieved and
starting to get excited. She phoned Jim right away.

"Hey, it's me. Guess what?" Rose said when Jim picked up.

"We got the apartment!" Jim said.

"Yes! How did you know?"

"Just a wild guess."

After talking for a few minutes, Rose and Jim decided
that Rose would fly down in mid-August for a four-day long
weekend to meet Mr. Rideout, check out the apartment,

pick up the keys, and meet Lulu Rose, who would be two months old by then. Jim would stay in Toronto, search for movers, and start packing.

As the summer progressed, Rose became more confident about relocating. The humidity and smog were unbearable. The last week of July, Rose and Jim gave their notice to their landlord, and Rose decided it was time to share the news with Kelly. She had already told Alison, who thought they were making the right decision and who promised to visit on a family vacation the following summer.

Rose decided to tell Kelly on a Friday afternoon, so she would have the weekend to think over Rose's proposal. When Rose knocked on Kelly's office door, she looked up from a pile of page proofs on her desk and waved her in.

"This issue is a killer," Kelly said wearily, looking at the proofs.

"We'll get through it," Rose answered encouragingly. "We always do."

"You're right, of course," said Kelly. "Although I don't know how I'd ever do it without you, Rose."

Uh oh. Rose cleared her throat nervously.

"Kelly, there's something I need to talk to you about," Rose began, shifting uncomfortably in her chair.

"Is everything all right?" asked Kelly, her tortoiseshell Dior reading glasses sliding down the bridge of her nose.

"Everything is fine. But I do have some news…"

"Are you *pregnant*?" asked Kelly, interrupting Rose before she could finish her sentence. Rose should have guessed that's what Kelly would have expected her news to be. "Because you know what a good maternity-leave package the company has. Although please don't feel you have to take the whole year off just because it's offered. You could take a few months and Jim could take the rest. Yes, I think that would work out nicely for everyone."

This was turning out to be harder than Rose had anticipated. Kelly was on a roll, but Rose had to tell her, so she spat out the words.

"I'm not pregnant, Kelly. Jim and I are moving to Halifax in October."

There! It was finally out in the open. Rose braced herself for her boss's reaction.

"Why ever would you want to move there?" asked Kelly. For her, living in a place that didn't have a DKNY was a fate worse than death by public hanging. As long as she was allowed to dress in her designer duds, she would face the rope with dignity.

"Jim was offered a promotion, and he's being transferred to the company's new office," Rose explained. "Plus, I have family there."

Kelly knew that Rose was from the East Coast, but she didn't take much of an interest in her employees' personal lives. Thanks to the relationship Rose had with her mother, that didn't bother her too much.

"But what will I do without you?" cried Kelly, when the reality of what Rose had just told her sank in.

That was Rose's golden opportunity.

"Actually, I've been thinking a lot about that. Here's what I propose—you keep me on the payroll as a regular part-time contributing editor and writer, since I can do those jobs by email. Then you can hire a freelance copy editor to come in and proof layouts during the production stage, since that's the only thing you really need a warm body in the office for." Rose waited while Kelly digested the plan.

"What about issue planning?" asked Kelly.

"You can conference call me during meetings, and we can do the rest by email and phone. Most of the time that's how we do things here, anyway. You know that days can

189

go by when we don't step foot into each other's offices, and sometimes I work from home when I'm writing." No matter what obstacle Kelly threw in front of Rose, she was determined to counter it with a solution.

"Hmmm, I don't know. I wouldn't be able to offer you health benefits or paid vacation," said Kelly, tapping her pencil on her desk and eyeing Rose to see if that was enough to discourage her from leaving.

"That's okay, I'll be on Jim's health plan, and I don't intend to take more than two weeks' vacation my first year of freelancing anyway, and I'll work them around the magazine's production schedule." Rose would miss her four paid weeks of *Dash* vacation, but never mind.

Rose saved the best bit, which she had been rehearsing for days, for last.

"Here's the thing, Kelly. I love working for this magazine, and just because I'm moving doesn't mean I can't keep doing that. The arrangement might change, but my commitment certainly won't."

Rose knew that sounded like she was sucking up—and maybe she was, a bit—but the funny thing was that she was sincere. She did love working for *Dash*, and with people telecommuting full-time from home for all kinds of companies, surely they could make it work.

Rose waited while Kelly considered her proposal. Finally, she spoke. "Let me think about this over the weekend, and we'll talk again on Monday."

Rose was dismissed as Kelly returned to her paperwork. At least she had one thing to be thankful for—Kelly hadn't said no.

Seventeen

ON MONDAY, KELLY ACCEPTED ROSE'S PROPOSAL, which meant she'd be guaranteed part-time work. They still had to negotiate the details and agree on a salary, but there was lots of time for that. In the meantime, Rose was going to start contacting magazines and newspapers in Halifax to line up interviews for when they arrived.

That morning, Rose booked flights for the second weekend in August, leaving Friday morning and returning Monday night. She would rent a car at the airport, drive into the city to meet Mr. Rideout and give him the security-deposit cheque, visit the apartment, pick up the keys, and then spend three nights with Daisy. She couldn't wait to meet Lulu! She had already bought her some presents, mostly Baby Gap clothes. To be fair, she had also bought gifts for the other kids, so her bank account was strained. She figured that it was only money, and they'd only be little once. Besides, if she ever did have children, she could take back all of the things she had bought Daisy's kids over the years.

On the first Saturday of September, Rose and Jim planned to host a farewell barbecue on their deck. It wouldn't be a big bash: Jim's friends and his favourite people at the advertising agency, including his boss, Chris, and his wife, Fay; the *Dash* girls (except for Kelly, who didn't think that management and staff should socialize outside the office); Michelle, Troy, Jenna, and Jeremy; Rose's hairdresser, Kaitlin, and her new boyfriend, who sounded normal and lovely; Vincente and Paulo; Dr. Davies; and Dr. Belliveau and Heather and their kids.

Rose wasn't planning to invite Charlotte Wright because she knew she didn't socialize with clients, so instead she booked a final therapy session a couple weeks before moving day, when Rose would say goodbye.

Suddenly, an idea struck Rose like a bolt of lightning. Fortunately, she was still standing and not lying flat on her back half-incinerated under a tree in a grassy field. Rose would add one more person to the party's guest list: their plumber, Harry.

⁂

On the Thursday night before Rose's scheduled departure, she packed her suitcase, confirmed her flight for the next morning and spent more time than usual talking to Jim before they went to sleep. The Friday-morning flight was uneventful, and when the plane touched down on the tarmac two hours later, the sun was shining. Rose made her way to the rental-car booth after she had picked her luggage off the carousel.

With car keys and suitcase in hand, Rose prepared to hit the highway. It was a beautiful mid-August day, and Rose turned on the radio. She had googled the location of the apartment, which was where Mr. Rideout would be waiting. Half an hour later, she turned onto a tree-lined street and parked in front of a big two-storey house with blue wooden shingles. A tall man with short silver hair was sitting on the front steps reading a newspaper. When he saw Rose get out of her car, he smiled.

"Hello, Rose!" said Mr. Rideout, striding purposefully toward her and shaking her hand. "It's nice to meet you. How was your trip?"

"Fine, thanks. It's a beautiful day here."

"This is God's country," said Mr. Rideout. "I was born and raised out West, but when I came to Halifax to teach a course fourteen years ago, I didn't want to leave."

Like the downstairs tenants, Mr. Rideout was a retired university professor; he had taught in the English department at Dalhousie University before retiring and investing in this rental property. Rose had a feeling that they were going to get along fine. He toured her around the place, which had been renovated recently. She could hardly believe that in just two months, she and Jim would be living here.

After Mr. Rideout gave Rose two sets of keys and she handed him the security-deposit cheque—and he shook her hand firmly again—she got back in the car and got ready to head for Daisy's house. Twenty minutes later, Rose pulled into the driveway and honked the horn. Ella, Katie, and Ryan came barrelling out of the front door—her three musketeers.

"Auntie Rose, we have a new *baby*!" they hollered in unison as Rose stepped out of the car. Rose wondered if they would always be this excited to see her. Probably not, so she planned to enjoy it while it lasted.

"I know! Do you like her?" Rose asked them.

"Yeah, she's pretty neat," said Ella. "But she doesn't do much yet, just eats and sleeps mostly. She's only two months old."

"I've been helping give her a bath," said Katie importantly.

"You have? You're a great big sister."

"I'm not da baby no more," said Ryan, who didn't seem as excited about Lulu as the girls did.

Rose crouched down to Ryan's level and hugged him.

"No, you're not the baby anymore. But do you know what?" Rose whispered in his ear.

"What?" Ryan whispered back.

"You're still the only boy," said Rose.

Ryan's eyes lit up. Then he started running around in a circle.

"I da only boy! I da only boy! I da only boy!" Ryan shouted, waving his arms wildly and heading for the front door so he could share this breaking news with his parents.

Rose stood up and smiled. Then she went inside to meet her new niece.

Lulu Rose had tiny rosebud lips, dainty hands, sweet-smelling skin, and a light fuzz of brown hair. She was awake when Daisy put her in Rose's arms, snug in her cotton sleeper, and a warm glow swept over Rose as looked into the baby's clear blue eyes.

Then Lulu peed on her aunt.

At first Rose wondered if Lulu had peed as a result of the thrill of meeting her namesake for the first time, like an excited puppy's involuntary reaction when it's introduced to new people. Rose watched as the dark stain spread over the left leg of her beige capris.

"Isn't she wearing a diaper?" Rose asked Daisy.

"Of course she is, but sometimes they leak," replied Daisy, laughing.

"Well next time use two, plus some duct tape!" said Rose, handing her to Steve.

"Don't worry, it means she likes you," said Daisy, wiping the tears from her eyes. "She's peed on all of us, too."

"How reassuring," Rose said, laughing too. "In which case, I hope she likes Jim when she meets him."

After lunch, they spent the rest of the afternoon in the backyard watching the kids splash in their wading pool. Daisy looked great and said Lulu was a good sleeper so far. Rose had texted Jim to let him know that she had arrived safely and that the apartment was amazing; he was packing boxes and had found an affordable moving company online. He had booked them for nine o'clock on the last day of September, and they had promised to deliver their stuff the following day by suppertime. Rose and Jim would stay at an airport hotel the night before they got on their one-way flight out of Toronto and into their new lives.

Rose slept well that night at Daisy's, and the next thing she knew the phone was ringing upstairs. She picked up her watch: six o'clock! The kids wouldn't even be up yet. Who was calling at that hour? Suddenly, Rose thought about Jim. What if something had happened to him? She jumped out of bed and ran up the stairs in her pyjamas. Daisy was in the kitchen holding the receiver to her ear.

"Yes. Okay. Right. I'll call you before we leave. Bye," said Daisy before hanging up.

"That wasn't Jim, was it?" Rose asked, trembling with anxiety.

"No, it wasn't," said Daisy, who looked dazed. "It was Mom."

"Mom? What did she want? They're not coming to visit this weekend, are they?" Rose hadn't told her parents that she and Jim were moving yet, and she had asked Daisy to let her do it when she was ready. They knew that she was staying with Daisy that weekend, but Rose had told them that she was coming to meet Lulu.

"No, she's not coming up. We're going to Wolfville," said Daisy.

"We are? Why?" Rose hadn't planned to see her parents this time, so there had better be a good reason for the visit. There was. During the night, John had suffered a heart attack.

☙

After Lulu woke up and Daisy fed her, the three of them hit the highway. Ella, Katie, and Ryan had wanted to go too, but Daisy explained to them that Grandpa wasn't feeling well so he couldn't have many visitors, which would make him tired, but when he felt better they would all go see him.

"That's not fair," said Ella stubbornly, sticking out her lower lip. "Lulu gets to go."

"Lulu will probably sleep the whole time, so she won't disturb Grandpa," said Daisy.

"What if she cries?" asked Ella.

"Then I'll take her out of Grandpa's room," said Daisy.

"What if I promise not to disturb Grandpa?" pleaded Ella.

Daisy stopped trying to reason with Ella, kissed her on the top of her head, and said she would give Grandpa a special kiss from Ella.

"Is Grandpa going to die?" asked Ella.

The nurse in Daisy didn't believe in shielding her kids from the truth.

"Grandpa is going to die someday, but I don't think it'll be this weekend," said Daisy. "After the doctor has told us how he's doing, I'll call Daddy and he can tell you how Grandpa's feeling. How does that sound?"

"Okay," said Ella.

On the drive down, Rose mentioned to Daisy that she was surprised that it was John and not Joanne who had suffered a heart attack. Rose told her about their mother's phone call, when she had admitted to having chest pains. Daisy was surprised, since Joanne hadn't mentioned it to her. An hour later, they arrived at the hospital. Rose parked as close to the front door as she could, and the three of them went inside.

John was in a private room on the third floor. Daisy knocked softly and pushed the door open. He was lying in bed with his eyes closed, an oxygen tube in his nostrils. Joanne was sitting in the chair next to him holding his right hand.

"How's he doing?" whispered Daisy, walking over to peer at the heart monitor.

"*He's* doing fine," said John, opening his eyes. "Hi, Daisy. Hi, Rosie. What are you doing here? Where's Jim?"

"I should be the one asking you the questions," Rose scolded him as she went over to hug him gently. "I'm down for the weekend to meet Lulu, remember? Now it's my turn. What are you doing here?"

"He didn't listen when the doctor told him that his cholesterol was high and he should stop eating ice cream and start exercising, and now here he is, hooked up to tubes and monitors and causing a fuss," said Joanne, who sounded annoyed but was on the verge of tears. Rose was sure that it had been a long night for both of them.

Daisy went to find the doctor, and Rose sat in the chair on the other side of John's bed. He looked pale, but otherwise he seemed okay; he said that he wasn't in any pain, which was a positive sign. A few minutes later, Daisy returned.

"The good news is that it was a mild heart attack, more of a warning, really," Daisy relayed.

"What's the bad news?" Rose asked.

"That Dad is going to have to start taking his health seriously," Daisy said, looking him in the eye and giving him her stern nurse's gaze. Then she ticked the following points off on her fingers. "That means you're going to have to give up ice cream, start exercising, and cut back on work."

When Daisy said that last part, Rose swore that a look of relief crossed her father's face—and one of despair crossed her mother's.

"Welcome to retirement, Dad," Rose said, smiling.

"Well, semi-retirement, anyway," John said, sneaking a sideways glance at his wife.

When visiting hours were over and John was nodding off to sleep, Daisy, Lulu, and Rose went back to the Ainsworths' house, where they'd sleep. John was going to be in the hospital for one more night so his doctor could monitor his vital signs before he was released on Monday. They'd stop in to see him tomorrow morning and then make their way back to Daisy's after lunch. Rose was going to be exhausted when she got back to Toronto.

Good Lord! Rose had forgotten to text Jim before they left Daisy's house. When they arrived at John and Joanne's, she did so right away and he called her. When she heard his voice, her heart swelled.

"Hey, honey," said Jim. "Steve called me this morning to tell me about your dad. How's he doing?"

"He's okay—he was really lucky," said Rose. "Things have to change when he goes home, though, or there'll be a next time and it'll be more serious."

"I'm sure he'll look after himself," said Jim. "Are you going to tell your mother that we're moving?"

"I hadn't planned on it—everything happened so fast— but it might not be such a bad idea now that I'm here," said Rose.

"I think it's a good idea," said Jim. "I'm sure she'll be pleased."

Rose wasn't so sure. After she and Jim had said good-night, she hung up and returned to the living room. Daisy was bathing Lulu. Joanne looked weary.

"Can I get you anything, Mom?" Rose asked.

"No, I'm all right, thanks," said Joanne. "It was a rough day, though. I have to admit that I was a little frightened. When I looked at your father in that bed, all I could think of was that it could have been me."

"It could still be you if you don't do something about your high blood pressure," Rose said.

"I know. I'll make a doctor's appointment next week. I guess your father and I have to admit that we can't keep up such a frantic pace," said Joanne.

"I'm glad to hear you say that. There's certainly no shame in reducing your schedules if it means you'll be healthier." Maybe John's medical crisis would end up being positive for both of them in the long run.

"I have something to tell you," said Rose. "Jim and I are moving to Halifax in October."

"You are?" Joanne raised her eyebrows. "What brought this on?"

"He got a promotion at work and a transfer," replied Rose.

"Tell him that I said congratulations," said Joanne. "Is it what you want, too? What about your job?"

There must have been something wrong with Rose's hearing. She thought her mother had just asked her two personal questions. Rose was glad that she was sitting down. Her father's heart attack must have really shaken Joanne up.

"I'm going to keep working for *Dash* part-time, and I'll try to get some local work, too," Rose said, trying to sound positive. The truth was, although she loved the idea of freelancing, it was going to be challenging.

"Well, you know I'd be happy to hand all of the company's copywriting over to you," Joanne said. "We can't find someone we like, and your pasta brochure was wonderful. Since your father and I are going to start spending less time at work, I could use your help. But only if you're interested."

Rose was floored—she hadn't anticipated that request, or her reaction to it. She had enjoyed writing the pasta brochure. It was a tempting offer.

"Can I think about it and call you to discuss it after I get back to Toronto?" Rose asked.

"Yes, of course. Now is definitely not the time to discuss business. In fact, I'm ready for bed. Thanks for coming today, Rose." As Joanne walked past her daughter, she stopped suddenly, bent down, and kissed the top of her head, like Daisy had done to Ella.

Who was this strange woman, and what had she done with Rose's mother? Because Rose was too tired to try to figure it out, she went to bed, too.

⁂

The next morning, John looked better. He had more colour in his cheeks and he was charming the nurses, which meant he was on the road to recovery. Daisy spoke to his doctor again, who said that John would be released the following day and sent home with a prescription for blood thinners and strict orders for a change in diet and lifestyle. After Daisy and Rose promised to phone him to check on his progress that night, Daisy, Lulu, and Rose left.

By two o'clock, they were back in Halifax. Rose was so exhausted, both physically and emotionally, that she had to nap before supper. In the evening, the kids snuggled with her on the couch as they watched *The Lion King* for the hundredth time. Rose read each one a story and tucked them into bed. Then Daisy called the hospital and spoke to Joanne, who was about to leave for the night. She said that John was feeling better, and she'd be taking him home in the morning. She sounded more upbeat. Before Rose went to bed, she watched Daisy nurse Lulu. Without question, Daisy was a wonderful mother. And Steve was a great dad.

On Monday after Steve went to work, everyone else went to Crystal Crescent Beach. Before they left the house, Daisy made sure they were covered in sunblock and that the kids were wearing sun hats with wide brims. Daisy and Rose sat at a picnic table in the shade with Lulu and watched Katie and Ryan make a sandcastle while Ella collected seashells and rocks. After yesterday's upset, it was a peaceful morning.

In the afternoon, Rose did laundry and repacked her suitcase, then called to confirm her flight. Next she texted Jim to tell him that everything was on schedule, and that her father had gone home that morning. She couldn't wait to put her arms around her husband, which is exactly what Rose did when they reunited. "Did you miss me?" she said, holding Jim tight and planting her lips on his.

"Of course I did," Jim said.

Jim felt good; strong and solid. Rose thought about her mother in the hospital room, holding her father's hand. She knew if anything like that happened to Jim, she would have a hard time bearing it.

"You've got lots of emails," said Jim.

"I do? From who?"

"Some of them are from Kelly, but there's one in particular you might want to look at sooner rather than later," said Jim.

Since Jim wouldn't elaborate, Rose went to the office and turned on the computer. She logged on and clicked on the email icon. Yes, most of them were stories that Kelly had sent for her to review. One of the other messages, however, made Rose suck in her breath.

It was from Sharon.

Rose ran out of the office and into the living room.

"You could have warned me!" Rose cried, punching Jim lightly in the arm. "Never mind Dad, I nearly had a heart attack just now."

"Sorry, I thought it would be better for you to see it for yourself," said Jim

"I'm afraid to open it."

"Why?"

"What do you think she wants?"

"I have no idea," said Jim. "Do you want me to read it first?"

"Would you?" asked Rose. "Don't read it out loud, just tell me if you think it'll upset me. Then I can prepare myself."

"All right." Rose followed her husband into the office and sat on the sofa bed while Jim clicked on Sharon's message. He was silent for several seconds.

"Hmmm," Jim said finally.

"Well? Does that mean it's good or bad?" asked Rose.

"It's interesting. Want me to read it to you?"

"No, but do you think I can handle it?"

"I'm pretty sure you can. Would you like to be alone when you read it?"

"Thanks, I think so."

Jim kissed Rose before he left the room. Rose took his place in the computer chair and faced the screen—and the music.

Dear Rose,

I've wanted to talk to you for a long time but I've been too afraid to pick up the phone. I still am— that's why I'm emailing instead of calling (cowardly, I know). I heard that you and Jim are moving to Halifax, and I thought it was time to try to make things right.

The first thing I want to say is that when I got your email right after Lauren was born, I wasn't myself. A couple of weeks after you sent it, I was diagnosed with postpartum depression. It was a difficult time, but I eventually came out of it. Then, much to my surprise and delight, I got pregnant again quite quickly. I'm pretty sure you heard that I miscarried. I wasn't clinically depressed after that, but I went through another rough patch. I'm pregnant again, and things are good so far, but I'm still scared something might go wrong.

I'm not telling you this to excuse my behaviour. You were right—I was self-absorbed, and I'm sorry about that. Since then I've realized that having a baby isn't the only thing that matters to me. I still need my friends. Unfortunately, you chose to share your feelings during a time when I wasn't able to cope with them. I realize now that you were in a tough place, too, and that neither of us could be there for each other. Maybe we can be now.
Love, Sharon

Rose had been waiting for that message for a year. It explained a lot. She was planning to sleep on it and decide how to respond in the morning, but instead she went with her gut instinct. Rose hit reply and typed:

I've missed you, too, Sharon. I accept your apology. I'll call you tomorrow night.

Then she pressed send.

The next night, as promised, Rose phoned Sharon. The call was awkward at first, probably because both of them were nervous. It turned out that as soon as Rose had left town on Sunday, Joanne had phoned Sharon's mother to tell her that Rose and Jim were moving, knowing full well that Sharon's mother would tell Sharon. Sharon's mother must have told Joanne that Sharon and Rose had fallen out, but Joanne hadn't said a word to Rose about it. Rose liked the fact that her mother wasn't always poking her nose in her personal business, but there were times when she wished she would.

It was good to talk to Sharon again. She asked Rose lots of questions—about work, yoga, Jim, and their move. Rose asked her about Lauren, Peter, and her pregnancy. It was almost like old times, only different. Better.

Eighteen

THERE WAS SO MUCH FOR ROSE AND JIM TO DO to prepare for their move that the rest of August flew by. They packed boxes in the evenings after work and arranged for power and phone hookups at their new apartment. When the end of August drew near, Rose started to plan their farewell party.

There wasn't much to organize. Everyone was going to bring drinks and whatever they wanted to grill on the barbecue. Rose was going to use paper plates and plastic cups and utensils so cleanup would be easy. After all, this party was about people, not things.

The Saturday of Labour Day weekend was beautiful, hot but not sticky or smoggy. By suppertime the temperature had dropped a few degrees, and it was comfortable on the deck. Rose and Jim made sure they had enough water, soft drinks, and condiments, and then they waited for people to show up.

And show up they did—every person they had invited came. As Rose looked around the deck at the people who felt like family, she got cold feet about moving. How could she leave everyone behind? She would be uprooted without them. Then Rose looked at Jim, who was talking to Chris and holding his and Fay's baby boy. That's when she knew they were doing the right thing. After carving out a successful career for herself in Toronto, now it was Jim's turn. Besides, if it didn't work out, they could always come back—no plan was irreversible.

Rose's eyes swept across the crowd, and that's when she realized that not everyone had come after all. Harry wasn't there.

Rose saw Rima talking to Alison, Yuki, and Michelle. She looked lovely; her hair was piled high on her head, her cheeks were flushed and she was wearing a simple but flattering pink slip dress. Where was Harry? Rose had called him a couple of weeks ago to invite him, and he had said that he'd come.

After the barbecue, a few people headed home. Michelle and Troy packed up the kids and started out for their cozy nest in the suburbs. Jenna cried and clung to Rose's leg before she left, and Rose made her promise to come visit them, which cheered her up. Then Jim's friends left. As he was showing them out, the doorbell rang—it was Harry.

"I didn't think you were going to make it!" said Rose.

"I know, I'm so sorry," Harry apologized. "My last job took longer than expected, then I had to go home and shower."

Well. He *did* look nice. And he smelled nice...

Rose shook herself. "I'm glad you're here," she said. "A few people have already gone home. Are you hungry?"

"Starving," said Harry. "I brought burgers."

Rose led Harry upstairs and took him out onto the deck. She introduced him to everyone, leaving Rima to last.

"Harry, this is Rima," said Rose. "We work together at *Dash*. Maybe the two of you can chat while I grill the burgers." Rose couldn't be sure, but she thought she noticed a gleam in his eye when he looked at Rima.

Off Rose went, leaving Harry and Rima alone. While Rose was flipping the burgers, Jim appeared next to her.

"Are you playing matchmaker tonight?" Jim asked.

"I just made the introduction," said Rose. "The rest is up to them."

By midnight, the last of the stragglers, including Harry and Rima, had gone home. Rose and Jim cleaned up, then collapsed into bed.

"That was a great party," said Jim.

"It was, wasn't it? We have good friends. I'm going to miss them." Then Rose started to cry.

"Aw, now, don't do that," said Jim, wrapping Rose tightly in his arms. "They'll come visit. And we'll make new friends."

Jim was right, but transitions were hard for Rose. Once they got settled, it would be easier for her to move forward. Right now, all she could think about was what she was leaving behind.

The next week, Rose went for her last session with Charlotte. They discussed how Rose felt about moving—sad, excited, scared.

"I have to ask you this before you leave," said Charlotte. "Have you and Jim made a decision about having a baby?"

"No," said Rose simply.

"Are you okay with that?"

"Yes. For now."

"That's great news," said Charlotte, smiling.

"What's great about still being undecided?" asked Rose.

"That's not what I was referring to," said Charlotte. "What's great is that you've reached a level of acceptance about something you can't figure out. Not everything in life is black and white, Rose. There are many shades of grey— you just have to pick one and make your peace with it."

"But do you think I'm overanalyzing things?" asked Rose.

Charlotte smiled. "My experience is that many women don't think long or hard enough about having a baby. I think you're right to consider this decision so carefully, because it isn't one that should be made lightly."

It dawned on Rose that her fear of the overwhelming responsibility of motherhood might always be greater than her desire to have a child. Recently it had occurred to her that perhaps the love and the fear go hand in hand. Maybe when you have a child, you're always a little bit worried.

That combination of love and fear might just be too much for Rose to handle. If she still felt this way a few weeks before her fortieth birthday, she'd be all right. She'd just treasure her time with her nieces and nephew.

When the hour was up, Charlotte walked Rose to the door and hugged her.

"Good luck," said Charlotte. "Please feel free to send me an update."

"I will," Rose replied, hugging her back.

As Rose stepped out onto the street, she felt a lightness radiate throughout her body. She was ready for the changes that lay ahead.

Acknowledgments

Six years have flown by since I self-published my first novel, *The Pregnant Pause*, in 2017. At that time, I couldn't have imagined that in 2021, Vagrant Press would publish my second novel, *Fishnets & Fantasies*, then "adopt" *The Pregnant Pause* and welcome it into their wonderful family of books. I have my editor Whitney Moran to thank for that, and I'll be forever grateful to her that even more readers will be able to follow Rose Ainsworth's journey from my first novel to my third one, launching in fall 2023 (if you enjoyed *Fishnets & Fantasies*, some of those characters will make a comeback in it, too).

Did you notice *The Pregnant Pause* has a cool new cover? I have designer Jenn Embree to thank for it!

What follows are the original acknowledgments I published when I first pushed Rose and her story out into the world. My gratitude hasn't waned.

⁓

Thank you to Edward Michalik, who didn't give up on his long journey to earn his PhD and who encouraged me to dust off my manuscript and have another go at it. You have a novel in you too, Ed.

It takes a village to self-publish a novel—a village of talented people working hard for very little (sometimes just a free lunch) because they believe in you and your project, and because they're generous and good. A massive thank you to Elizabeth Eve for saying yes when I asked if she wanted to read my manuscript, and for her solid suggestions, steady guidance, and soothing presence throughout; Nadine Arseneault for her creative and colourful cover concept; Rachael Kelly for her photographic and digital prowess, her eagle proofreading eye, and her cover input; and Brenda Conroy for turning all of the various elements into this book, at the speed of light, no less. *The Pregnant Pause* wouldn't be here without them.

I owe an enormous debt of gratitude to my "first readers," who took time out of their busy schedules to read the final draft of my manuscript while it was still a Microsoft Word document, then wrote nice things about it: Janice Biehn, Sue Comeau, Ann Douglas, Laura Earl, and Charlotte Empey. Each of you is an accomplished writer—thank you for "all your words."

To my colleagues at the Schulich School of Law at Dalhousie University, especially Lindsay Loomer for her tales of mothering young children in her forties and for listening to me talk about my book during our workday; Karen Kavanaugh for helping choose the chapter-heading style and reviewing cover options, designing a poster, and making me laugh ("Get my coat! Not *that* coat!"); Chrystal Harrigan Gray for her side-splitting spontaneous storytelling; and Rob Currie for understanding firsthand the challenges of juggling a creative sideline.

It would have been difficult to write this book without the inspiration of Eleanor Scott, Sarah Munroe, and Matthew Munroe. Cheers to them and to their makers, Anne and Bil Scott and Clare and Hugh Munroe.

For their encouragement, I offer heartfelt thanks to Sue Comeau for promising not to be "that kind of mother" (you aren't!) and for her valuable self-publishing insight and social media support, Amy Pulsifer for cheerleading and offering to hawk books with me at the farmers' market, Anne and Doug King for their objective cover consultation, Sunita Sharma and Jackie Snooks for sharing motherhood stories, Rebecca DeCoste for helping spread the word, Angie Brooks for empowering me at one of the low points, Liz Mazerolle for her neighbourly interest, and Ann Wetmore for her wise counsel.

I'm grateful to Renée Horton of Horton Publicity for working hard to source a broad readership and for writing a damn fine press release.

It isn't possible to mention everyone who has shown support for *The Pregnant Pause*, but you know who you are—I'm mentally inserting your names here.

Thank you, Craig Pothier, for your steadfast support and patience during my manuscript's resurrection, for being a great sounding board and my very first "first reader," and for telling me partway through that you were enjoying it and I was a good writer—I'm still buoyed by those words. I'm also grateful for your All My Words logo-design suggestion when I was too tired to make any more decisions, and for absolutely everything else that you do.

Thanks most of all to my co-creators, Richard and Mary Ann Doucet, for having a baby who grew up to be me.

NIKI DAVISON

JANE DOUCET is a journalist whose articles have appeared in myriad national magazines, including *Chatelaine* and *Canadian Living*. In 2017, she self-published her debut novel, *The Pregnant Pause*, which was shortlisted for a 2018 Whistler Independent Book Award. Jane is thrilled that Vagrant Press has re-released *The Pregnant Pause* with a fresh new cover. In 2021, Vagrant published Jane's second novel, *Fishnets & Fantasies*. Jane's third novel, *Lost & Found in Lunenburg*, publishing in 2023, combines characters from her first two novels. Jane lives in Halifax, Nova Scotia, with her husband. To learn more about Jane and her books, visit janedoucet.com.